SHOULDA

A SECOND CHANCE FOR MR. RIGHT

PEPPER NORTH

Pepper North
With a Wink Publishing, LLC

AUTHOR'S NOTE:

The following story is completely fictional. The characters are all over the age of 18 and as adults choose to live their lives in an age play environment.

This is a series of books that can be read in any order. You may, however, choose to read them sequentially to enjoy the characters best. Subsequent books will feature characters that appear in previous novels as well as new faces.

You can contact me on
my Pepper North Facebook pages,
at www.4peppernorth.club
eMail at 4peppernorth@gmail.com
I'm experimenting with Instagram, Twitter, and Tiktok.
Come join me everywhere!

PROLOGUE

In the beginning

Third grade began as all years did. A class full of unique personalities and abilities burst into a cheerfully decorated room to meet their teacher and see who would be in the same class. In one particular classroom, students paused at the doorway looking for the new teacher at school. Would she be nice or strict?

Their worlds were upended when they found a quirky-looking male teacher wearing a big bow tie. Meeting them with a big smile, Mr. Chamberlain encouraged everyone to find the desk with their name on it. Clumped together in small groups, the students slowly slid into their assigned seats.

Maisie, Amber, Harper, Beau, and Colt discovered they were group five, arranged the farthest from the teacher's desk. Despite the boys giving each other cootie shots when they found out they were sitting with girls, the group bonded quickly and spent the rest of the year begging him to let them remain together. Thankfully, the phenomenal teacher responded to their good behavior and positive support for each other and hadn't separated them.

. . .

HARPER – Senior year of High School

When her name was called, Harper turned toward the door. She definitely didn't want to sing in front of this packed crowd. Colt wrapped an arm around her waist and growled into her ear.

"Come on, Angel, I can't do this without you. Help me celebrate, Harper."

"There are so many people."

"Just concentrate on me, Little girl."

Her gaze locked with his and saw the encouragement and caring in his eyes. "I hate you for making me do this," she protested.

"Come on. You'll love me when the music starts," he answered confidently.

Snorting quietly, Harper focused on the worn flooring in the bar as he coaxed her up on the small stage. Held against his powerful frame, she refused to look at the faces that stared at them. He was pure hotness and toned muscle. She knew she looked ridiculous next to him. Harper knew she outweighed him by thirty pounds, at least.

The lyrics flashed on the screen, and she forced herself to take a deep breath. His "you've got this" reassured her almost as much as the familiar music. She loved this song and hated it at the same time. Launching herself into the riveting female solo at the beginning, Harper heard the quick intake of breath from those crowded closest to her.

This was one thing she did well. Sing. She'd always loved to sing— but in the shower, in the woods, or alone with her friends at a campfire. Performing in front of other people scared her badly. Harper relied on Colt's strength as he held her steady at his side.

She relaxed a slight amount as his rich tenor voice joined hers. The crowd spontaneously clapped in appreciation. Harper glanced up at Colt and found him in the zone, making eye contact with their audience and soaking in their enjoyment. He was a complete entertainer— a combination of devastating appearance, incredible voice, charm, and the undefinable star quality. He made her tingle inside, and she'd even seen him taste the wintergreen paste back in elementary school.

That thought made her laugh inside and more of the tension ebbed from her body. Feeling it, Colt rewarded her with a squeeze of his arm as he sang just for her. Harper hadn't asked him about his plans after high school yet. She knew he wasn't ready to decide to accept an athletic scholarship at their state university. Colt seemed to wrestle with some other option he hadn't shared with her yet.

He will when he's ready.

Harper would make it through high school with the help of her friends and specially chosen classes. She toyed with taking a few business classes at the local community college next year. Her joy in life was children. Not school-age kids but little ones who smelled like baby powder, or the grass they trampled on unsteadily in the yard.

While she babysat all the neighborhood kids, Harper dreamed of opening her own childcare center—something small at first but expanding as she could. Kids were her life. She loved them whether they giggled at her lame jokes or screamed with a skinned knee. Harper knew she could make a difference for them, and she was determined to be the best second mommy to everyone she cared for.

The song ended with a reprise of her solo that had launched the song. Harper channeled all her dreams and hopes for the future into the lyrics, allowing her voice to swell into the notes. When the final sound faded out, there was absolute quiet for two seconds before thunderous applause filled the bar.

"Damn, Angel. Together, we're unbeatable." Colt's rough voice slid over her, drawing her gaze to his handsome face.

"You're the star, Colt. I just make you sound better."

Harper watched his expression harden and knew he didn't care for her words. The crowd interrupted them with demands for an encore and she quickly keyed in a tune that required two male voices. Waving Beau up to take her place, she fled from the stage to rejoin Maisie and Amber. Ignoring the feel of Colt's gaze on her, she chatted with her friends as the masculine tones blended together. Beau's voice was good. Colt's voice was incomparable.

Two weeks after high school graduation

Why won't she come with me?

Colt shoved his last pair of jeans into the suitcase. He was angry at her, angry at himself, and filled with self-doubt.

When a knock sounded at his bedroom door, he growled, "Leave me alone, Mom. You and Dad were very thorough in telling me all the reasons I shouldn't believe in myself."

"I believe in you," a sweet voice observed, making him whirl around.

Harper stood framed in the doorway. Out of his cherished circle of friends dating back to that first day of third grade, she was the one dearest to his heart. As much as he treasured Beau, Maisie, and Amber's friendship, Harper had always been the one for him. He'd always thought they'd be together—until now.

"Did you come here to try to convince me not to go?" he asked angrily.

"No. I know you're going. You're supposed to go. I came to spend a few last minutes with you. I'm going to miss you so much," Harper shared with tears in her eyes.

Colt shook his head, trying to maintain his resolve. He had to try this even though it felt like she was ripping his heart from his chest. He turned to grab some socks from the drawer and slammed it shut before turning to face her again.

"Then why the hell don't you come with me?" he demanded.

"I'll just hold you back," Harper whispered.

"That's bullshit and you know it. We're supposed to be together. You're supposed to be with me."

"How sure are you that going to Nashville is your path?" she asked, coming in to sit on his bed.

Immediately, he sat across from her on the opposite side of the double bed. "Four hundred percent."

"I believe you. I know this is what you have to do."

"Come with me," he asked, reaching for her hand and squeezing it gently.

"I can't, Colt. As confident as you are that you need to leave town

4

and try to make it as a country superstar, I know my place is here," she told him.

"You could open a daycare anywhere," he pointed out.

"If only I could, but I need to be here. I'm not like you. I'm… petrified of being in a new place that I don't know how to get around in, with no one I know to help me," she shared.

"I'd be there," he assured her.

"You would be. I know you'd always be there for me. Unfortunately, that will take your focus off doing what's important for you to succeed. We both know I'm great at a lot of things, but I'm too gullible."

"Kind-hearted," he corrected her.

She smiled at his editing. "I don't function well in crowds. My heart pounds and I want to cry. That won't go well with performing in front of a stadium of people."

Harper held her hand up when he opened his mouth to argue. "I might get better at being in public with you in time, but this isn't my dream. It's yours."

Colt stared at her for a second and digested her words. She was right. This was what he wanted. Her path was completely different. "I'm sorry, Harper. I'm an idiot."

"You are not. You're focused. That's what's going to help you make it big. I can't wait to see it happen. I am your biggest fan," she told him.

"You're so much more than that, Little girl."

"I can't be your Little girl, Colt. That's why I always say 'no' when you ask me out. You'll be a great Daddy to someone."

"You are my Little girl. We've been together since before we even knew the name for this bond between us. I'm not going to forget you. When you're ready to be mine, all you have to do is call. I will be there so fast there will be burnt rubber on the road into town."

"I can't count on you coming back, Colt. That's not fair to you. You need to go explore and live your life."

Harper looked around the room, seeming desperate for something as tears cascaded down her cheeks. Reading her mind, Colt bolted from the bed to snag a box of tissues from his desk and set it in front of her.

"I don't want you to cry, Harper. How can I make this better?"

"Fast forward twenty years or so. My heart will have recovered by then," she joked, wiping away the moisture under her eyes.

"You can always change your mind. I'll come get you," he promised her.

"Thanks. I'll remember that. I won't do it, but I'll remember you wanted me with you."

"Always. I'll always want you with me," he corrected her.

Harper dashed away a few tears and said, "You're leaving tomorrow?"

"Yes. I'll leave at eight in the morning. You can still change your mind and come with me. There's still time."

"I won't change my mind, Colt. It's not the best thing for me or for you."

Harper stood and took a step toward the door before hesitating. She turned to face him. "Could I have a hug?"

"You're breaking my heart," he said, rushing around the bed to wrap his arms tightly around her. Unable to stop himself, he tangled his fingers in her hair and pulled her head back. Capturing her lips in a kiss, he poured out all his love for her and his frustration that they couldn't be together.

Her hands braced against his chest and Colt was ready to release her at her first move away. He'd never pushed himself on her and he never would. Her fingers grabbed his shirt. Colt felt the rasp of her fingernails through the fabric on his skin as Harper clung to him. Instantly, he was hard as he wrapped one of his arms around her waist to pull her soft curves fully against him.

Colt memorized everything—her taste, the feel of her body against his, the way she responded to him. He was ready to call off his plans and stay here with her forever. He tightened his hold on her automatically when she shifted away.

"You have to let me go, Colt," she urged, tugging backward.

"I don't want to, Harper," he confessed before relaxing his arm around her waist.

"Sorry." He moved back six inches, searching her face to make sure he hadn't scared her.

"I wanted that kiss as much as you did, Colt. I'm going to miss you so much."

Covering her mouth with one hand, Harper whirled and dashed through the door. Colt automatically took several steps after her before bracing himself on the door frame to halt his progress. Chasing Harper would only make it harder and postpone the inevitable.

CHAPTER 1

"*D*on't you get lonely taking care of everyone else's children?"

Miranda's expression clued Harper in immediately that she was taking out a bad day on her favorite target. The former head of the dance squad in high school seemed to love making others feel bad to make herself happier. Harper had ignored the jabs for years, hoping Miranda would just leave her alone. It hadn't happened yet.

"Never!" she answered the carefully maintained woman as she finished cleaning up a puddle of spilled liquid from the floor and refastening the sippy cup lid more securely.

"There you go. Want to go play with the blocks?" she suggested to the toddler before standing to gather Cinderella's things for Miranda. Harper always cringed at her name. The spoiled child definitely hadn't been a princess when Miranda enrolled her.

"Cinderella had a few accidents today. I'll send her extra clothes home with you. Just bring a few more back in case she has challenges again," Harper suggested.

"I don't know why you can't just wash the dirty ones and hold on to them," Miranda groused, holding the cloth tote Harper handed her far from her beautiful leather coat.

"I know you want to do as much as you can for your daughter," Harper assured her.

"I'm fine with you washing her clothes," Miranda answered with a smirk.

"Sorry, Miranda. That's not part of the contract we have signed."

Harper turned to approach a small group playing nearby. She coaxed the girl from the play group with her usual cheerful 'time to go home' song she'd created for the kids. Even their sweet giggles couldn't stop Harper from rolling her eyes at the gall this woman had when she faced away from Miranda.

The two most prestigious daycare centers in town had already kicked out her former classmate for treating the staff like her personal servants. Harper had only allowed Cinderella to come to her smaller facility because she wanted to help the terribly overindulged child learn how to make friends. She was under no illusions that she'd be able to make a tremendous impact on Cinderella's life, but if she could offset some of the traits that characterized her mother…

"No home. Here," Cinderella babbled when the quick tune was over and fussed as Harper led the toddler to Miranda.

"You stopped calling her Cindy, right?" she asked, setting down the bag to scoop her daughter up in her arms without a word of greeting.

"Of course, Miranda. After your correction, I always call her Cinderella," Harper answered with a forced smile. She looked at the vicious woman holding the babbling child. Crossing her fingers behind her back, Harper hoped to have some effect on how Cinderella treated others when she got older.

Miranda turned to walk to the door, but stopped to turn back to look at Harper. She tapped her fingers against her lips before saying, "The reunion is coming up and I know you don't want to attend alone. There were people talking about you last time. You know, you're single fifteen years after school and never even date."

"Miranda, I don't think you need to worry about my love life," she said quietly, hoping that would end the conversation.

"I don't think you qualify as having a love life, Harper. All you do is take care of other people's kids. I worried about you being bright enough to care for Cinderella, but she'll be in school before any lack of mental stimulation puts her behind other students."

"Let me assure you, Miranda, that all the children in my care have a wide variety of experiences and interactions. I've done my research to make sure that everyone learns as much as possible during their time with me. It would help if you would support my efforts. Tomorrow, everyone is bringing something that starts with the letter D. Have a conversation with Cinderella about things that start with a D."

When Miranda looked at her blankly, Harper continued, "You know; dog, doughnut, dime, dinosaur…"

With a hiss of exasperation, Miranda interrupted. "I know what starts with the letter D. I didn't barely make it through high school."

"High school was a long time ago, Miranda."

"I know. That's what brings me back to what I was trying to discuss with you when you rudely shut me down. I thought of someone who would love to take you to the reunion. His name is Rufus."

The only person she knew named Rufus flashed into her mind as Harper stared at her in astonishment. Surely, this was a joke.

"Are you talking about the homeless guy you have living outside your building?"

"I'm only trying to help. He was very excited to escort you."

"You've already asked him…" Harper stopped in the middle of that sentence to take a deep breath to control her anger in front of the children before addressing Miranda.

"While I'm sure you would be happy to have someone take him in from the street so you don't have to worry about him discouraging clients from visiting your knickknack store…"

"Collectibles, Harper! Besides, it's not like you have anyone wanting to date you—much less marry you. He might even have sex with you. Some men do like obese women."

"Miranda, I'm going to ignore what you just said to me. Please, leave," Harper said, stiffening her spine.

11

"Oh, come on. You're the perpetual virgin. What are you saving yourself for? Colt? That weird relationship certainly fizzled when he left town."

Pissed beyond thinking clearly, Harper blurted, "Colt and I are closer than ever now." Miranda didn't need to know that their private conversations over the years had always ended with Colt asking Harper to marry him. Of course, he'd been kidding each time.

"Really?" Miranda said, raising one eyebrow.

"Of course. Colt is very dear to me. Back to your date suggestion, I do not intend to date, sleep with, or anything else with Rufus, so you'll have to find some other way to remove him from your sidewalk."

"I don't know why I even bother being nice to you. You just refuse to take good advice," Miranda interrupted Harper with an exasperated expression. She turned, stalked to the doorway, and dug an envelope out of her pocket. "Oh, here's your pay this month. There are only twenty weekdays in February, so I prorated the cost down."

"Miranda, your bill I gave you last week has the correct amount. Also, you were late seven times this month in picking Cinderella up. There is a fee for that." Harper chased her to the door, carrying the bag of soiled clothing Miranda had abandoned on the floor.

"You're here anyway," Miranda said with a sneer.

Taking a deep breath, Harper said the phrase she'd been practicing since last month. Now, thanks to Miranda's attempts to further shortchange her by lowering the basic monthly rate, she'd have to address that. "There is no prorated amount for the month and if you are late, there is a penalty. I'm sorry your shop isn't making enough money to pay the full daycare bill, but the policy is the same for all parents."

"My shop is doing wonderfully," Miranda gasped with affront. "I'll bring you a check tomorrow."

"With an item that starts with D," Harper reminded her, trying to school her face not to smile as the unpleasant woman backed down like her mom had told her she would when they practiced the reference to her shop's income.

"Fine." Miranda reached out and snatched the bag from Harper's extended hands.

"And Miranda? I already have a date for the reunion. Colt is taking me."

"Colt Ziegler? He hasn't been back for a reunion yet," Miranda stated with a skeptical look at Harper.

"This year, he'll be there. With me." Harper crossed two more fingers behind her back.

"We'll see." Miranda let herself out the door.

* * *

THANK goodness the next mother walked in a few minutes later to distract her. The flurry of parents claiming their children occupied all her focus. When the center was empty, Harper cleaned and disinfected all the surfaces on automatic pilot as she forced herself to concentrate on what enrichment activities she'd offer the children tomorrow.

On her way out the door, Harper hesitated and looked back into the small daycare. She loved this place. It had come onto the market at a ridiculous price when she'd finished all her classes and started looking for a space to make her own. After having her parents help her check it over completely, she'd stopped questioning the bargain it provided.

Thanks to a granduncle she didn't even know, whose lawyer had contacted her with an inheritance of a chunk of money, Harper had the funding to invest in her own center. When she'd gotten a grant to purchase equipment and supplies, Harper hadn't questioned how the charity had found her. Each year, that charity sent her money to enrich the environment for the children in her care. Good luck had definitely supported her well. She closed and locked the door carefully.

Once in her car, Harper tried not to panic. Colt was actually planning on coming to the next reunion. Why did she have to insinuate that they had something so much more? Before she could stop herself, Harper selected his number and pressed the call button.

"Harper! I wasn't expecting to hear from you, Little girl. What a treat!" Colt's beautiful voice cascaded over her like the best caramel syrup ever made.

"You may not think so when I tell you what I did," she confessed.

"What's up?"

"Miranda..."

"What's the bitch done now?" he demanded.

"I'm afraid I'm the bitch this time."

"I doubt that seriously. What's going on, Angel?"

"She wanted me to take the homeless guy who lives in front of her store to the reunion."

"That sounds like Miranda. You said no obviously."

"I did, but she kept pushing me. Made fun of the fact I'm a virgin and asked who I was saving myself for. Your name came up in our conversation. Before I knew it, I'd told her you were coming to the reunion this year. There's nothing that's come up to keep you away, is there?"

"I will be there and I'll be glad to be your dedicated escort to the dance."

"Could you...act like you're attracted to me?" she asked, blurting out the rest of the question.

"You want to fake being in a romantic relationship?" he suggested, and she could hear amusement in his tone.

"Don't laugh, Colt. I wouldn't ask except I backed myself into a corner with Miranda and I hate that she always gets to belittle me."

"No one gets to make you feel bad, Angel. I will be there. You can count on me."

"Thank you, Colt," Harper said, wiping away the tears that had run down her cheeks.

"There is one thing wrong with your plan."

"Really? What?" she asked, gripping the steering wheel a bit tighter.

"I'm not acting."

"You're not acting? I'm sorry, I don't understand."

"I was attracted to you in the third grade. Leaving you after graduation about killed me."

"That was a long time ago, Colt. You hang out with gorgeous, famous people now. I'm just one of the friends you hung out with in high school," she corrected him.

"You were never simply a friend, Harper. I will see you at the reunion and I will enjoy showering you with affection."

"Don't make it, like, goofy."

"You have a lot of conditions on this relationship we're entering. I'll have some of my own," he told her with a stern tone that thrilled her.

Don't take his words the wrong way. Harper forced herself to laugh as if he were joking. "I'll definitely owe you big. Thank you, Colt, for helping me put Miranda in her place—at least for a weekend."

"You really should stop caring for Rapunzel."

"Cinderella, Colt!" Harper laughed, knowing he was mixing up the princess names on purpose.

"I can't get there until the reunion. I stacked everything before the gathering so I could stay in town for a while. Can you keep your chin up until I get there in a few weeks?"

"Yes. She only flares into annoyance about once a month. She'll be too busy picking on someone else for a while," Harper answered with a sigh.

"Oh, and we're going to talk about all the other stuff later."

"We are?" she asked, mentally reviewing everything she shared with him.

"We are, Little girl."

CHAPTER 2

"*W*oohooo!" Colt celebrated by lifting his bass player off his feet and twirling him around in a circle before setting him down and dancing to the piano.

"What has gotten into you? Are we up for a country music award?" the other musician demanded.

"Probably, but that's not why I'm excited. Harper called."

"Harper, from your hometown? The one you write every love song about?"

Colt grinned at him and trailed his fingers over the piano keys. "That's the one."

"We figured she didn't exist," the backup singer added.

"Oh, she exists," Colt assured them.

"When is she coming to Nashville?"

"Never. I'm going to her."

"Appledale? I don't think you'll fit in there anymore," the bass player scoffed.

"Avondale," Colt corrected absentmindedly as he made plans. "I'll be fine."

"Are you quitting music?" the drummer asked.

"Never. I'll divide my time between there and here." Colt looked at his band and noticed the concern written on their faces. "Music is who I am. I'm not planning to stop recording and writing songs. I'm probably going to rely on you more than ever now. I'll keep this place and build another studio in Avondale."

"What are you going to do? Fly us to Avondale to practice?" the bass guitarist asked with a laugh.

"Yes. I guess I need to look into private charters. We'll figure this out if you can continue to work with me. Are you all able to help me make this work?"

Colt looked around at every face that made up his team. He knew his success didn't just rely on his talent, but the magic they made together. His gaze locked with each person to let them know they were important. Their nods went straight to his heart.

"Thank you. Let's make some music," he suggested. "I've got a month to wait. Think we can finish this album so we can all take some time with the people we love?"

"We're just waiting on you," the bass player ribbed him.

Within a minute, they all were immersed in the project they'd been working on. When he wasn't singing, Colt had a tune playing in the back of his mind. They needed one more song for the album, but it had eluded him. He'd have a late night ahead of him. Inspiration had struck again, and he knew it would be good.

* * *

THE DAYS PASSED in a flurry of activities. About a year ago, a well-known, wealthy landowner in Avondale passed away. Colt had jumped on the opportunity to buy an enormous slice of the property old man Howard's heirs dumped on the market. He'd sat on it for a while. Now, not only was he working on music, but Colt searched for an architect and landscaper.

For a couple of weeks, he jotted down his requirements for the design. When he finished the list, Colt expected the architect to run the opposite way.

"I know this is a lot to organize on the property," Colt apologized.

"Definitely. I'm going to want to experiment with this project. There's no problem with the quantity of land you own. We can put all of this and more into that space. I'm assuming you'll want some distance between the house and these other features," he suggested, pointing at the other areas Colt had detailed.

"The house needs to be as private as possible. That's my priority. The second is providing the key location for this area," Colt said, pointing to one detailed column. "A private gated entrance for each grouping is important as well."

"Got it. Well, you've given me a challenge and I love them. Give me a couple of weeks and I'll have something roughed out for you. Then we'll tweak the plan until my drawing fits all your criteria and makes you happy."

"I'll want my fiancée to have a look at it as well," Colt said, loving the way that French word rolled off his tongue.

"Of course. Will she have other ideas I need to incorporate?"

"I don't think so. But it's possible." Colt hedged his answer. He didn't think Harper would be unpleased with anything he'd planned, but Colt wanted this to be her house as well.

"I encourage you to work together on the plan. I'd be glad to meet with you both when I've got a rough outline. Modifications during the planning stage are fairly easy to accomplish."

"Sounds good. She's in another city. I bet we could look at it on a video call."

"Definitely. Where's the property?"

"A small town far from Nashville."

"Do you have a builder?"

"Not yet. That's on my list," Cole confessed. "Any recommendations on what to look for when I select one?"

"Definitely. I have a set of screening questions I recommend people ask. If you send me the address of the property, I can check our nationwide database for names of builders in that area," the architect offered.

"Perfect. I'll send that information as soon as I get home."

The architect took another look at the requirements Colt had listed. "It's unusual to have a large room accessible only through the master bedroom besides two walk-in closets. For safety, would you consider a door?"

"I would prefer that it be isolated completely. If on the ground floor, a window could serve as an emergency exit."

"This is not a space for a minor?" the architect probed.

"No. It is a private space for my wife and me." Colt met the man's gaze directly from across the desk. He got the impression from his last question that the architect knew exactly what they would use this space for. He was sure other clients had requested many different types of designs and special needs.

"I understand. If I run into other questions, would you prefer that I call, email, or text?"

"Send me a text. I'll get back to you as soon as possible." Colt stood and offered his hand.

As they shook hands, he noticed a picture on the man's desk of a beautiful woman wearing cat's ears and holding a fancy teacup. Immediately, he thought of a tea party for a Little and her Daddy. Colt filed that plan away. There were so many things he wanted to experience with Harper.

"My wife, Margie. She is the love of my life and keeps me hopping."

"How long have you been married?"

"Sixteen years. Our wedding was right after our college graduation. And you?"

"Our wedding will come soon," Colt answered vaguely.

"Best wishes. I'll be in contact with the plans."

"Thank you."

CHAPTER 3

*H*arper tried every outfit in her closet on three times and visited the only store in the small town that carried plus-size clothing twice. She considered ordering something online, but nothing ever fit her right and she'd learned to try on clothes before buying anything.

Propping her hands on her hips, she stared into the mirror. This sundress would have to do. It flowed over her generous bottom and belted in to fit her narrower waist. Maybe it took five pounds off her appearance? *Who am I kidding?*

Carefully, she took off the dress and hung it back in her closet. She'd wear that one to the Friday night reunion social gathering at Murphy's and hope it looked suitable. She still needed to find a fancy dress to wear to the more formal dinner and dance.

Maybe she could put together a couple of things. She had a black skirt that she could jazz up. With the right top, it might look okay. Harper dug through the clothes in the limited dressy section of her wardrobe. No. No. No.

There was nothing there that would work. Since it was Saturday, she was free from everything. Harper decided to drive to the next larger city and hunt for something she could wear.

Crossing her fingers, she gathered her phone, purse, and keys to take on the mission.

As she drove out of town, Harper passed the road famous in her high school days as the trek to the party spot. The last owner had been working with a developer to clean up the area when he'd passed away. When old man Howard's sons and daughter had settled the estate, they'd put that area up for sale.

Harper had contacted the realtors to see if they would sell a small parcel of land on the corner, separate from the rest of the property. Unfortunately, they'd decided to wait for someone who was interested in a larger portion of the property. There was no way she could have afforded any more space. Maybe when the new owner took control, she could sweet talk them into selling her the corner space.

She spent the rest of the trip daydreaming about how she would design her dream daycare center. It would have to be bright and colorful with lots of toys. A washing machine on the premises would be handy so she wouldn't have to haul the crib sheets and stuffies home to wash. Lots of built-in storage and flexible play areas would be fantastic with a playground outside.

Harper knew it was a pipe dream. She'd never be able to afford anything like that. Her income was limited. Running a small center for children wasn't lucrative, and she always spent extra money on the kids instead of sticking to the strict budget she'd designed.

Approaching the city limits, she pushed the thoughts from her mind and focused on what she needed now—a top to make her feel confident and sexy. That wasn't too much to ask, was it?

She parked at the mall and headed inside. Several shops later and finding nothing, Harper paused in front of a new shop in the mall. A pleasant-looking clerk working inside met her gaze and smiled. Decision made, Harper risked walking inside.

"Hi!" she greeted the friendly employee.

"Hi! I'm Patsy. Just browsing or is there something special you're looking for?" the young woman asked.

"I'm not sure if you carry anything in my size?"

"Of course we do! What do you need? A fun, casual outfit or something special?"

"I need something for a dressy event," Harper confessed.

"Come over here and check out these dresses. There are several I'm in love with," the clerk confided. "Let's see what suits your taste."

Harper felt her heart beat faster. Could she really have a choice of several instead of settling for something just okay?

Soon, she stood in the midst of several racks of sparkling outfits. Harper crossed her fingers behind her back. *Please let something fit.*

Thirty minutes later, she had three outfits picked out. How was she going to decide? She looked helplessly at Patsy, who had made the shopping trip so much fun.

"I don't know either," Patsy commented, reading Harper's mind. "Are you sure you won't need more than one?"

"No…" Harper didn't want to leave any of these here for someone else. She didn't even feel guilty about it.

"Want to choose your favorite and I'll write down all the information about the others so you can come back to pick them up later if you change your mind? I can't guarantee they'll still be here, but the clerk on duty could help you find out more easily."

Harper's phone buzzed, and she looked down at the screen to see a message from Colt. He'd sent her at least one message every day since she'd called him in a panic. Nothing heavy—just random questions or details about his day. She loved hearing from him.

"Let me think about it for a few minutes while I answer this text," Harper requested, waving her screen at Patsy.

"Of course. There's no rush. Want me to check if the manager will give you a special deal if you take all three?"

"That would be amazing. Thank you," Harper said, and felt her anxiety build once again. Financially, she shouldn't buy the dresses, but she wanted them so bad.

She opened the message to read:

Hi, Little girl. I wanted you to know that I'm thinking about you and that there are 27 more days until I'm there. What color dress are you wearing to the fancy event? I'll try to pick out something complementary.

What a coincidence! I'm standing here trying to figure out which of three beautiful dresses to buy. I never have luck shopping like this.

Buy them all, Little girl.

I'm not on a country star budget, Colt. Besides, I won't ever wear all three. What's your favorite color? Blue, green, or ivory?

She almost dropped her phone when it buzzed in her hand. Answering it quickly, she asked, "What's wrong?"

"Not a thing. Hand your phone to the clerk. I'll take care of this for you. You need all three. I plan to wine and dine you," Colt's amazing voice directed.

"I don't need all three. We just need to pretend for a couple of nights and then you can disappear back to Nashville," Harper reminded him.

"I'm not pretending, Harper. Hand your phone to the clerk."

The steel in his voice made her walk to the cash register where the saleswoman waited.

"Did you decide on which one?"

"I'm supposed to hand you my phone," Harper said, feeling her cheeks flush with embarrassment.

"Hello?" Patsy said into the phone. "Yes, sir. I'm glad to take care of this for you."

Harper listened to one side of the conversation and tried to fill in what Colt said.

"Does she need anything else? Definitely some undergarments, and jewelry would help finish the look. You'll take care of the jewelry? Yes, sir."

Patsy handed Harper back her phone. "He knows you're panicking. I'm supposed to let the two of you talk while I gather a few extra things for you."

Accepting her phone, Harper stammered, "Colt, you can't do this."

"Of course I can. It will make me happy to spoil you a bit. I don't think anyone does that for you, do they?"

"No. But I don't need to be spoiled," she answered quickly.

"Every Little girl needs to be spoiled," he stated firmly. "I want to do this for you. It will make me happy. You want me to be happy, don't you?"

"What a question, Colt! Of course I want you to be happy. But you can be elated without buying me things I won't ever wear."

"You'll get to wear them, and I'll get to see you in them. It's a win-win. There's no debate. If you don't let me buy them for you now, I'll call the shop and have everything shipped to your house."

She knew when she'd been overruled. "Thank you, Colt. This is very generous of you."

"Not generous. Totally selfish. I've wanted to take care of you for twenty years. It's you who are doing me the favor."

"Colt..."

"Pass the phone back to Patsy, Little girl."

Without another word, she handed the phone back to the sales-clerk. Patsy soon had everything rung up and charged to Colt's credit card. A large shopping bag and three hanging bags waited for Harper.

As soon as she'd completed the transaction, Patsy said into the phone, "Thank you, Mr. Ziegler. Can I say how much I love your music?"

She soon disconnected the call and handed it back to Harper. "He said he'd call tonight. You just made my day. I got to talk to Colt Ziegler. His voice is amazing. Almost as phenomenal as you look in these dresses. I'm so glad you get to take all of them home."

"I wasn't expecting him to buy all this," Harper commented, waving her hand over the bags.

"I did give him the discount the manager allowed me to ring up. We saved him a few bucks," Patsy confided.

Their gazes met, and both women laughed. Like Colt Ziegler needed to save any money.

"It must be exciting to date him," Patsy said.

"We're not really dating," Harper rushed to correct her.

"You're dating. No man buys all this for someone they don't care about deeply. No matter how much money they have. I'd offer to help you carry things out but I'm the only one here right now," Patsy apologized.

"I can carry it. I'm stronger than I look. Thank you for your help, Patsy. I love these dresses."

"Come back and shop again. We have some cute casual clothes as well. I'm here Saturday through Tuesday during the day."

"I'll be back."

Harper arranged the packages in her arms and headed for the door. Passing all the stores that hadn't carried clothes for her, she felt like a proverbial princess. Colt shouldn't have done this but she'd dress up for him. He might not even notice.

"He'll notice," ricocheted through her mind. Colt had always looked at her like a tasty treat he'd love to devour.

Maybe I should let him and pretend I don't know that heartache will follow when he moves on.

Harper pushed that thought out of her mind as she set the parcels in her trunk. Even Cinderella took a risk for one night and it worked out for her.

But Cinderella only had ugly stepsisters. I have Miranda.

To her surprise, that thought didn't have any power. Harper really didn't care what Miranda thought right now. She'd bask in her time with Colt and deal with the repercussions later.

CHAPTER 4

"Thank you so much for coming to read, Mr. Chamberlain," Harper said on Monday afternoon when her all-time favorite teacher filled in as the guest for story time when the parent who had signed up for that day didn't arrive.

Of course Miranda hadn't troubled herself to come.

"Anytime, Harper. I'm so glad to see you and meet the kiddos lucky enough to be in your care. I brought my favorite book, if that's okay?"

"Of course. They'll enjoy something new."

Harper turned to the children who gathered behind her to see who the visitor was. "Story time!" she announced and herded everyone to the story nook.

It always took a few minutes to settle all the wiggling bodies into a good spot. Mr. Chamberlain sat down in the chair in the middle and talked to the children, helping Harper lure them in for a quiet pause to their play. She smiled at him as he carefully retied one toddler's shoe and chatted knowingly about the cartoon character on the boy's T-shirt. The retired teacher certainly had a way with children.

She retrieved a fussing baby from a crib to feed her a bottle as Mr.

Chamberlain read the enchanting story of a bunch of kids on a wild adventure. Harper found herself as captivated by the story as the youngsters sitting on the floor at his feet. She enjoyed having a book read to her as much as the toddlers did, especially when read by someone as dynamic and fun as her former teacher.

When it was over, he answered a wide variety of questions from the toddlers. There were even some about the book, confirming that they'd paid as much attention to the story as Harper had.

"That was fun. Thanks for inviting me."

"Thank you so much for coming. I'm sorry for the last-minute request," Harper told him.

"My pleasure. Call anytime. If I'm not substituting, I'm glad to come. This place makes me happy. It's filled with positivity and love," Mr. Chamberlain said with a fond smile.

"What a compliment. That's exactly how I want it to feel."

"You're doing a great job here, Harper." He paused before continuing a bit more quietly. "Are you taking care of yourself as well as you're tending these youngsters?"

"Of course. I love my work."

His eyes narrowed and seemed to look inside her. "Are you happy outside of work, Harper? That's important, too. I worried about you when all your friends left for college and didn't return. Do you still talk to them?"

"Of course. We've been bonded since your class. We video chat together at least once a month and we text back and forth," Harper rushed to assure him. "They're still my best friends."

"I'm glad to hear it. Is everyone doing well?"

"Maisie's doing some kind of research that I don't understand, but I'm sure it will advance medical treatment."

"You were all destined for great things. Don't discount your contribution. These children will enter school happy and well prepared to succeed at whatever they wish to do. I don't know the background of all the kiddos you watch over, but based on the odds, this is the only place they feel truly safe. That's all thanks to you."

"That's very nice of you to say, Mr. Chamberlain…"

"I'm a nice guy, but I hope you know I never lie without a purpose," he said meaningfully.

"Oh, I remember that discussion we had in class. How did you ever come up with telling us they were replacing you with another teacher? We were so angry," Harper remembered.

"I definitely had everyone's attention for that lesson."

"I swore never to lie from that point on," she told him.

"You were always a delightful student—worried about others' feelings and very compassionate. I don't think lying was your style even then," he complimented her.

Their brief window of being able to talk was over as the children, tired of sitting in the reading spot, demanded Harper's attention. She picked up a hungry toddler and bounced him on her hip.

"This is yours now," Mr. Chamberlain said, handing her the book that had enchanted everyone. "Call me again. And tell those friends of yours I'd love to see them sometime."

"I'll tell them. Thank you." She waved the book at him as she held it away from the child's reaching hands. Harper would place this book in her reserved section that only she could access.

She watched the door close behind the kind man before getting mid-morning snacks for everyone. What an impact he'd had on her life. Harper scanned the happy faces sitting at the table together, eating a nutritious treat, and suddenly felt great. Wrapping her arms around herself, she realized that her goal was always to be a Mr. Chamberlain—just in her own way.

Happier with herself than she'd been for a long time, Harper quickly tidied up the play space while she kept an eye on the snackers. She didn't realize that she was singing until Cinderella's warbled voice joined her. The other toddlers joined in with a babble of words. Where else could she sing spontaneously and have background singers pitch in?

This job rocks.

* * *

DURING NAPTIME, Harper contacted several friends in the daycare business. She'd need some time off on Friday before the reunion social gathering at Murphy's. To her delight, one of her friends had a daughter in town who would be glad to come cover the last two hours on Friday. Rose could also come the Friday before to hang out in the afternoon and meet the children and their parents as a practice run with Harper there. Rose had just returned to Avondale and enjoyed working at a daycare.

With that easily figured out, Harper breathed a sigh of relief. She would stress to the parents that they needed to pick up their kiddos on time, so Rose could close the center on time. Crossing her fingers, she hoped everything would keep working out so well.

Detailing the change in routine in her weekly email to the parents, she stressed the credentials of the substitute caregiver for the last few hours on that Friday. Some parents would decide to pick their child up early. Others would trust her judgment in selecting an appropriate substitute.

A change in routine is tough for everyone.

Moving quietly around the room, Harper cleaned and straightened. Her precious charges touched every surface and each other. Harper did her best to tackle the germs before they could spread between the children. She'd been sick over and over for the first year but had gained a super resistance to illnesses through the constant exposure.

Thank goodness, because she was awful when she was sick. Oh, she could force herself to go to work because only an emergency could make Harper close the daycare. She'd learned to work with a headache and other aches and pains. A mask adorned with a smile controlled any cough and cold germs as much as possible. But inside, she just wanted to curl up in a warm bed and have someone take care of her.

Frowning at that thought, Harper realized she had been alone for so long. Over the years, she'd dated a few men but never seriously. When Colt left, he took her heart with him.

Shrugging her shoulders to push off negative thoughts and coulda, shoulda, wouldas, Harper finished her cleaning before sitting down for a short break. There was a new book she couldn't wait to read. The main character promised to be a stern Daddy dom.

Just the way I like them.

CHAPTER 5

*H*arper tugged her dress into place after getting out of her car. Her older sedan looked conspicuous in the parking lot filled with the latest models of sports cars and SUVs with out-of-state license plates.

There are locals here, too, she reminded herself, noting cars she saw here every time she visited the pub. *It's not just my classmates showing how well their lives are going.*

Running a daycare wasn't the ticket to making a million dollars in twenty years—or in any number of years. She loved her work and wondered if everyone else could say that.

Feeling better about her life choices, Harper slung her purse over her shoulder and noticed a familiar redhead pulling into a space nearby. Amber hadn't seen her. As Harper approached, she could see her friend obviously concentrating on something.

Oh, no! She was *not* bailing.

Harper crossed the asphalt to knock on her window and smiled when Amber jumped in surprise. Her smile morphed into a laugh as her friend threw open the car door and jumped out to hug her.

"Amber, I've missed you so much!" Harper squeezed her friend super tight.

"We've been talking all the time online," Amber reminded her.

When Amber didn't seem to be in a hurry to get inside, Harper asked, "Have you talked to your folks recently?"

Making the decision not to share the big surprise waiting for her friend inside, Harper was relieved when Amber changed the conversation back to the reunion. That relief turned to self-consciousness as Amber scanned her appearance before looking down at what she was wearing.

"Do you think I look okay? I figured rumpled jeans are a fashion statement, but you look amazing. Did I miss dress-up requirements in the schedule of events? I know, I'll put on my vamp shoes. They're in the back," Amber decided.

"You look gorgeous in everything," Harper assured her, following Amber to the trunk.

As she watched Amber fancy up her outfit, Harper's inner worrywart fretted. Should she tell her or not? Finally, words burst from her mouth. "There's something you should know before you go inside. Want to call your folks and tell them you're here?"

Instantly, Amber looked at her with a laser glance. "You tell me."

Harper didn't want to be an uncooperative patient under Amber's care. That tone meant business.

Squaring her shoulders, Harper decided Amber needed to see this for herself. She nodded and answered, "Well… Let's go inside and get that daiquiri first."

"What in the world is going on? Are you okay?" Amber asked, immediately suspecting the worst. When Harper nodded, she followed with, "Is everyone else okay?"

Wrapping an arm around Amber's waist, Harper hugged her close and assured her that everyone was fine. While Amber processed her words, Harper steered her friend into Murphy's.

They scanned the room and saw a crowd on one side of the bar. Harper couldn't stop the giggles from tumbling from her lips when Amber whispered about how old people looked. She'd seen many of these people around town over the years and watched them age gradually.

"Feeling like that fairytale character who sleeps for a hundred years?" Harper asked.

"Wow! I hope everyone has a nametag. I don't recognize anyone. They all got old," Amber whispered to Harper as she looked around.

Harper knew the minute she saw the magnetic man behind the bar. She shifted away to watch. *Pure magic.*

For years, Rio had played a major role in Amber's life. It first began as an older brother-type who had always treated Amber as an adult rather than a preteen cheerleader. Harper had watched her friend's interest shift to having a crush on him to something so much stronger. When Rio disappeared, Harper had supported Amber to help her through her despair.

When Rio had shown up as the new owner of the bar, Harper had given him not a piece, but a chunk of her mind. She'd also listened to his answers and understood she wasn't part of this. She'd support her friend in whatever path Amber chose to follow. Secretly, Harper hoped for a magical happily ever after.

She liked Rio and understood why he'd left. Now, would Amber? Harper watched him vault over the bar and stalk forward to run his hands over Amber's shoulders and down her arms, as if he couldn't keep himself from touching her. The look on their faces was magical. It made her believe fairytales could come true.

When Rio walked back to the bar, Harper watched Amber shake her head as if trying to regain her footing after seeing the man she'd felt so much for after twenty years. Harper resumed her position next to Amber.

"What is going on?" Amber demanded.

"This is between you and Rio. Come on. Let's get our nametags. You can protect me from Miranda," Harper suggested as she led the way.

Miranda was in fine form, complaining about Harper having a substitute and refusing to be open on Saturday so Miranda would have the day and evening free for the reunion. When Miranda complained about the germs in the daycare making her daughter sick and added a thinly veiled threat to report Harper's daycare business to the city inspectors, Harper quickly stood up for herself, feeling Amber bristle next to her.

"There are regulations for all daycares, Miranda. The inspectors visit regularly. Perhaps you would prefer another daycare option. I'll miss Cinderella, but completely understand."

"If you weren't the cheapest place in town, I'd move her," Miranda snapped and Harper knew that the unpleasant woman had forgotten they had an audience. Thankfully this time, children weren't within listening distance.

Before she could answer, Amber locked gazes with the bully and commented, "Wow."

"Let's just get our nametags, Amber. It's okay," Harper assured her, seeing realization dawn in Miranda's eyes that others could hear the conversation. Talking to Miranda in private was always a negative experience.

Finding her badge, Harper slapped it onto her dress and watched Amber lean over the others. As her friend lifted hers from the table, Amber met Miranda's gaze directly and touched two spots on her hairline.

"Your facelift tape is coming undone here and here."

Harper tried not to laugh as Miranda immediately raised her hands to double check those spots, proving Amber's suggestion that Miranda had attempted to make herself appear less wrinkly was correct.

Leaving a sputtering Miranda behind, Amber and Harper stepped away. Before Amber could say anything to Harper about the encounter, former members of the cheer squad swarmed around her friend.

Harper stepped away automatically to allow them to get caught up on each other's life. To her surprise, they included her in the discussion. They seemed genuinely glad to catch up with her, as well as Amber.

Keeping her eye on Amber, she watched the former cheerleader's gaze lock with Rio's when the conversation shifted to reveal that Rio now owned Murphy's. It was as if they could communicate over the space that separated them. Harper covered her lips when they twitched with laughter upon seeing Rio shake his head at Amber and her shrug it off.

"Hi!" Monica appeared with her tray. She handed Amber a strawberry daiquiri.

"Harper, Rio sent you your favorite—a vanilla rum and diet Coke," the server announced, offering her a tall glass.

"Thank him for me, Monica," Harper answered.

"Ooo! Is that a strawberry daiquiri? I haven't had one of those for years. Let's go get one," Becky suggested. In a flash, they were back alone as the cheerleaders streamed toward the bar.

Amber's laughter drew Harper's attention away from the parade for strawberry beverages. Harper watched her turn to look at Rio with amusement. The two shared a long-distance smirk.

"What did I miss?" Harper asked with a smile. It was going to be so much fun to watch these two. *Maybe happily ever afters do exist.*

"He didn't put any alcohol in here. Rio always used to do that when I was a kid so I could have the cool drinks like all the glamorous women at the bar," Amber shared.

"You two have a lot of history," Harper said before noticing the arrival of two very special people.

"Look, there's Maisie and Beau. He picked her up at the airport," Harper said, pointing at the entrance.

With Amber on her heels, Harper rushed forward and greeted two more of their close circle of friends. Harper squeezed Maisie's slight figure close before giving Beau a bear hug. She only remembered at the last moment that maybe that wasn't acceptable anymore.

"Oh, sorry. Is hugging you off limits now?" she asked the handsome silver fox.

The entire group had always known Beau would follow his father into politics. Harper suspected there were new rules to follow now that he was in office.

"You can hug me any time, Harper," he assured her when Maisie suggested Harper was concerned about media coverage before pulling Amber close as well.

Harper had seen her friends over the years but couldn't stop staring at them. Maisie looked amazing. Gone were the threadbare hand-me-downs and in their place was an understated outfit that fit and complemented her perfectly. Even if Maisie had admitted to having a stylist now pick out her clothes, the brilliant scientist wore them with style.

And Beau. He exuded power and prestige without meaning to. Just as he had oozed leadership skills in the third grade, now he drew everyone's attention. She crossed her fingers, hoping they'd get some time to talk as a group privately.

Harper looked for the security and media that always encircled him on TV. "Did they let you out alone?" she teased Beau.

"I have Maisie. She'll protect me," Beau answered, wrapping his arm around the smallest of their group. They all knew that while petite, she was a honey badger at heart.

"Well, well, well. The gang's all here. Except for the famous country star. He's too busy to come, I guess. Even as Harper's imaginary boyfriend," Miranda sneered from behind them.

Maisie immediately put the unpleasant woman in her place. "Good grief, Miranda. Are you still so constipated that you treat people like shit?"

Harper tried to control her smirk as everyone turned to look as Maisie's voice carried around the room. Maisie definitely hadn't lost her blunt way of dealing with others. Quickly, she said, "Maisie, it's okay. I'm not sure why Miranda is worried about my love life."

Almost visible steam rose from the unpleasant woman's reddening face and Harper knew Miranda would exact her vengeance in the future. Sighing inwardly, Harper decided it was totally worth it. She let Miranda get by with too much because she didn't like conflict.

CHAPTER 6

$\mathcal{E}$veryone turned to stare as the door banged open and an enormous figure rushed in to Murphy's. Colt Ziegler stood at the entrance, scanning the crowd.

Damn, he looks good. Harper clenched her fingers into balls as she forced herself not to run into his arms as she wished.

A stellar athlete in high school, Colt had excelled in a variety of sports. On television specials and over their video calls, Harper had watched his teenage body fill out to become a grown man. Now seeing him in person, Colt's broad shoulders mesmerized her. She traced them lower as they tapered athletically to a trim waist. She closed her eyes for a moment to file that mental picture before looking at him again.

He's so out of my league. How could I ever expect anyone to believe that he's my boyfriend—much less Miranda?

Colt smiled as he found their group. Focusing on Harper, he strode forward. "Hi, Angel."

As soon as he reached Harper's side, Colt wrapped his arms around her, pulling her tight against his body. Pressing a kiss to her lips, he apologized, "Sorry I'm late."

When she moved automatically to cover her mouth in shock after his kiss, Colt captured her hand and pulled it to his mouth to graze his lips over her fingertips. Mesmerized, Harper stared up into his deep brown eyes. She knew this was totally pretend on his part, but she couldn't help enjoying every second of being pressed against his hard body. He felt so good.

The hush behind her made Harper turn her head to meet Beau's controlled features that didn't reveal his thoughts, Amber's shocked glances, and Maisie's wide mouth expression of astonishment. They were going to have questions. She heard Colt's low chuckle and squeezed her thighs together as the sound fueled the arousal that had flared into life the second he'd entered Murphy's.

"The tour bus driver got slowed down by the traffic on the highway," Colt explained. "I was about ready to jump out and run when it finally cleared. Thank goodness the rental place brought the truck to me to save time."

"You expect us to buy that Colt Ziegler is really your boyfriend, Harper?" Miranda interjected with a brittle laugh of disbelief.

"Sorry?" Colt looked at her with confusion written on his face. "Were *you* in our class?"

Harper kept herself from laughing as he even looked directly at her Avondale Dragons' graduate nametag. He was so good. Even Harper couldn't tell he recognized her name.

"Colt! I'm Miranda Teasdale. I led the Dragonettes."

"Weren't you the head cheerleader?" Colt asked Amber.

"Not the cheerleaders—the Dragonettes. I led the dance team," Miranda corrected him with offense dripping from her words.

"Oh. That makes sense. The dance team was on the field while I was in the locker room." Colt shrugged off her self-inflated importance and turned to extend his hand to Beau. His broad shoulders separated Miranda from the small group of friends.

"I guess you've got that Senate seat all wrapped up by now. I hear your name all over the news even in Nashville, Beau," Colt greeted him, completely dismissing the woman behind him as they shook hands.

"Wish me luck, Colt. I'm glad to see you in person," Beau said with a smile. "Seems like a very long time since I could lob the ball your way on the field and rely on you to catch it."

"I could still use you as a backup singer if the politics thing doesn't work out for you," Colt joked, making the group laugh.

Turning his attention to Maisie and Amber, he hugged them close before returning to wrap his arm around Harper's waist and asking them, "When are you finally moving home?"

When Harper tried to shift away, he tightened his hold on her and looked down to meet her gaze with a stern, silent message. Instantly, Harper subsided. *Yes, Daddy.* She almost giggled as that thought burst into her mind.

She forced herself to listen to the conversation as Amber shared the news about her new job at Avondale's General Hospital. "I can't believe you're going to be in town now. This is going to be so much fun. We can come to Murphy's together after work," Harper enthused.

"Not me. I'm still in the think tank in DC," Maisie added quickly before turning her attention on Colt. "And I don't think they'll let you out of Nashville."

Colt just smiled down at her. "Coming home sounds good now," he said, looking at Harper before drawing her in for another kiss. He had to glimpse the confusion and wonder on his friends' faces. Colt enjoyed keeping them on their toes.

"Have I missed something?" Amber asked as soon as Miranda drifted away with a snort of disbelief.

"Congratulate us. Harper finally agreed to be my girl," Colt answered before Harper could say anything. He was definitely not pretending anything for the other classmates at the reunion.

"Wow! I'm so happy for you. Why didn't you say something?" Amber asked.

"We needed this to be secret for a while. Now, we're ready to tell the world," Colt shared and rewarded Harper with a squeeze when she smiled shyly and nodded.

Before Amber, Beau, and Maisie could ask questions, a server approached with two microphones. "Rio sent me. I keyed up your favorite song from your senior year. Come sing for the crowd," she invited.

Before Harper could refuse, Colt accepted the microphones and steered her to the small stage. "Do this for me, Angel. I've wanted to sing with you for over seven thousand, two hundred and twenty days."

"How do you keep count of all of those numbers?" Harper said in disbelief, walking automatically at his side.

"When things are important, they stay foremost in my brain," he assured her. "Plus, I have a counter on my phone."

"You track how long it's been since we've sung together?" she asked as he helped her step up on the stage.

"That's important to me. Ready?" he asked.

Harper looked at the crowd surrounding them. Not only were there former classmates, but the regular crowd filled Murphy's. When Harper came for a drink, she didn't mingle with many, but the regulars recognized each other and were cordial. Most of that crowd had never heard her sing.

"It's been so long," she whispered.

"Sing for me, Angel," Colt urged, and she caved.

"Okay." Fixing her gaze on the words displayed before her, Harper didn't look at anyone.

The song demanded her attention. Opening her mouth to allow the vibrant notes to flow from her, Harper could hear the quiver in her voice. Colt's fingers intertwined with hers and squeezed tightly, reminding her he was here. She held onto him, absorbing his strength and support as she relaxed into the music. The challenge of something more demanding than children's tunes inspired her. This was fun!

When Colt's incredible voice joined with hers, Harper shivered. The blend of their abilities drew the best from them both. She peeked up to judge the reaction of the audience as the conversation in the bar dropped noticeably in volume.

Rapt expressions and smiles met her glance. They were all enjoying the music. Confidence grew inside her as people gathered around them. She knew most were eager to hear Colt sing. He was the star of their graduating class. But she also noted that her singing wowed the acquaintances she'd run into at Murphy's over the years. They'd never expected her ability to bring a song to life.

And her band of friends? Harper grinned at them as Maisie hooted her approval, Beau gave her two thumbs up, and Amber cheered her on. She sneaked a look at Rio behind the bar to find him dancing as he concocted drinks. He caught her eye and winked. Harper knew he was Amber's, but the gesture made her feel more appealing.

When Colt let go of her hand to wrap his arm around her and pull her hip tight against his body, Harper knew he'd seen it, too. She nudged him with her elbow to let Colt know he had nothing to worry about. As if anyone could be more appealing.

The last notes faded out and the crowd went wild. Asking her a silent question, Colt's eyes locked with hers. Harper hesitated and then realized that this could be her only chance to sing with him. Colt would have to leave again. She couldn't keep him there. When she nodded, he keyed up another song for them.

"That's my girl," he said quietly to her.

She couldn't stop the smile that spread over her lips. Being with him always felt so good. Harper crossed her fingers behind her back. *Please let time freeze now.*

After the next song, Colt waved to the crowd and invited another classmate up to entertain everyone. He helped Harper off the stage as their class clown stepped up eagerly to butcher a new popular tune, singing so badly that the crowd couldn't help being amused as the duo walked back to join their friends.

Loving the feel of Colt's large hand steering her through the crowd, Harper smiled up at him. "That was fun. Thanks for encouraging me."

"We'll do it again. I'll look forward to singing with you here again."

"The crowd didn't know it was going to get a Colt Ziegler concert tonight," she joked.

"Colt Ziegler, the country star, isn't here tonight. When I'm with you, I'm the same guy who sat next to you in Mr. Chamberlain's class."

"Mr. Chamberlain. How is he, Harper?" Maisie asked, overhearing the last of their conversation as they approached.

"He's amazing. I just saw him. He was a guest reader for my crew. They love it when he visits," Harper said with a smile.

"Is he still teaching?" Maisie asked.

"Yes and no. He's retired now, but he substitutes a lot. I'm sure he's in great demand to cover classes. He told me to tell you all he'd love to see you," Harper shared.

"I think that's a great idea. We don't really have time this weekend, but once we're all back in town, let's get together for lunch or dinner," Beau suggested.

"Great idea," Colt agreed.

A wave of classmates joined them as everyone mingled throughout the room. Colt kept Harper close to him. She let him answer everyone's thinly veiled and blunt questions about their relationship. A people person, Colt could handle everyone. It was a huge relief to allow him to take care of this. Harper would have never been able to answer all the questions.

"Want to get out of here?" Colt asked about two hours into the gathering.

"Oh, I don't want to miss time with everyone," Harper rushed to say after covering her mouth to hide a yawn.

"You're exhausted. What time were you up this morning for parents to bring their children into your center?"

"I usually get up at four to have breakfast, dress, and drive to the daycare. Parents start arriving at six. I've got a couple toddlers whose mommies and daddies work at the hospital. They have to be there early," Harper explained.

"It's time you were in bed. Let me see you home."

"I hate to cut our evening short but I am exhausted," Harper confessed before yawning again. "Where are you staying tonight? With your folks?"

"No. I'll get a hotel room."

"I overheard earlier that the hotels were full this weekend," she said, worrying.

"I can sleep in the truck I rented," Colt assured her. "It won't be the first time."

44

"I don't want you to do that. I have a couch if that's better?" she offered hesitantly.

"Thanks, Harper. I'll take you up on that offer."

Placing his hand on the small of her back, Colt steered her out of Murphy's. Harper allowed him to guide her through the door without argument. She'd normally say goodnight to their friends, but they would know she was safe with Colt. It would take the last of her energy to drive home.

CHAPTER 7

*H*arper rolled over to look at the time on her clock and froze. Colt was on the bed next to her. He lay on his side facing away from her. Glancing over his sculpted shoulder and back muscles, Harper swallowed hard when she reached the elastic waistband of his snug boxer briefs. She didn't know if she was happy or sad that he was wearing them.

Sad, definitely sad, she thought, scanning over the full, tight curve of his ass.

He was sleeping soundly. Harper tugged the covers over her back slowly to avoid shifting the covers trapped underneath him and waking Colt up. Sliding her legs over the side of the mattress, Harper tried to ease herself into a sitting position. The mattress springs squeaked slightly, and she froze in place, looking over at Colt. His breath caught and then settled back into its normal rhythm.

Harper caught herself breathing with him, willing him to stay asleep as she slowly stood. Smoothing her T-shirt over her thighs and tugging it lower, Harper inched toward the attached bathroom where her robe hung. Once there, she stared at the empty hook and remembered wearing it to bed last night and tossing it onto the side of the bed for the morning. The same side Colt now laid on.

She peeked out the door and could see bits of the flowery material hanging over the side of the bed. Not much—Colt's muscular form covered most of the robe. *Crap!*

Okay, she could put her coat on. That would work as a robe, right?

Peeking at the bathroom mirror, Harper shook her head. She needed to look better when he woke up. Before she abandoned the bathroom, she eased her brush off the counter and heard the teeniest click.

The mattress groaned, and she registered Colt's heavy steps coming toward the bathroom. Freezing, she looked around for some way to hide. Short of getting into the shower and hiding, she was caught.

"Angel," Colt called, his low voice husky with sleep. As he entered the room, he smiled and walked toward her, wrapping his arms around her waist and pulling her close to him.

Harper held her breath as he rested his head on her shoulder and stood, holding her against his body. When he did nothing other than squeeze her close, Harper inhaled. Warm masculinity filled her senses. His hard frame against her tantalized as his arms held her gently, yet securely. She could feel his morning erection pressing against her and reminded herself that he was hard for biological reasons, not because of her. Unable to resist, Harper tentatively wrapped her arms around his shoulders, unsure what to do.

"Good morning, Little girl," he whispered against her skin before he pressed soft kisses to the bare skin exposed by the wide neckline of her T-shirt.

Harper tried to stifle her moan of delight at the sensations as he trailed warm kisses up the sensitive side of her throat and over her jaw. She was not successful.

"Mmm, let me hear your sounds, Harper. Let Daddy know you're enjoying his touch," he instructed.

"Colt..."

Her words evaporated as his lips captured hers—first in a soft kiss, followed by a low groan of arousal that did things Harper had never felt. Colt deepened the kiss and dipped his tongue inside her mouth.

She abandoned any concept of control as she responded eagerly to the exchange. The feel of his hardness against her evoked a primal response that couldn't come close to the excitement already welling inside her.

This was Colt. The man she'd fantasized about for years as a teenager. His face still occupied her thoughts as she pleasured herself alone. Squeezing her legs together, she fought against grinding herself against him. Colt solved her dilemma, stroking one hand down her spine to cup her round bottom and pulling her closer to move against her intimately.

Harper curled her fingers into the corded muscles of his shoulders, trying to stabilize herself in the rush of all the sensations bombarding her. She tore her mouth from his. "Colt, I've never…"

"We're not in a rush, Little girl. There's no timeline or pressure. You've waited this long. You'll know when it's the right time for us to make love."

"We c-could," Harper stammered.

"Your body is ready now. Is your heart and brain?" Colt asked.

Hesitating, Harper searched his face, trying to figure out what to say. She didn't want Colt to be turned off by her body. He could have anyone he wanted. Why would he want her? And she really wanted to have her first experience to be with a man who was going to be around for a while. Not just a casual fling.

"You're thinking too hard, Angel. You're not ready until I've helped you resolve all the concerns floating around in your mind."

"Will that ever happen?" she blurted.

"We'll happen. When it's the right time."

He seemed to be waiting for her to answer. Harper stammered, "O-okay."

Brushing one hand through her blonde hair, Colt cupped the back of her head to pull her close. His kiss this time was sweet and tender, making her heart melt. When he lifted his head, the devastatingly handsome man looked deep in her eyes. "It's definitely going to be way better than just okay, Angel."

She nodded without consciously deciding to. When he chuckled, reading the surprised expression that followed her agreement, Colt said comfortingly, "It's okay, Harper, to let Daddy please you. That's what we've both always dreamed about." He pressed a light kiss to her lips and stepped back to push his briefs to the floor. Immediately, Colt stepped into the bathtub and pulled the shower curtain around his bulk. When he started the shower, she heard his sharp inhale.

"It will get warm if you wait a few minutes."

"I don't need a hot shower, Angel," he growled.

The giggle that slipped from her lips surprised Harper. When Colt pulled the top of the shower curtain back to look at her, Harper ran to the enclosed toilet area before she wet her panties laughing.

Harper had never considered how having fun together could be as bonding as sexual heat. Leave it to Colt to be the complete package: good looks, talent, success, a sense of humor, and oozing with sex appeal. After quickly taking care of business, Harper darted into the bedroom and stepped into fresh panties. Listening to the water still running in the bathroom, she decided she had enough time to finish dressing. Ripping her nightshirt over her head, Harper rushed to the dresser to find a bra with some style or sex appeal. Of course, she didn't have any. She heard the water turn off and grabbed the plain white cotton bra on top. Fitting her breasts into the cups, she twisted her arms around her back and tried to get it hooked.

Damn! Where are they?

"Let me help you, Angel."

Colt's low voice sounded even lower than normal from right behind her. He brushed her hands away and quickly fastened the garment. His cool hands stroked over her sides, making her shiver. He stepped forward to whisper in Harper's ear.

"I'm going to need a million cold showers if you don't get clothes on."

"I was trying," she babbled, wrapping her arms around her rounded stomach as she kept her back to him.

Capturing her hands, Colt pulled her hands down to her sides. "Never hide from me. I have always loved you exactly the way you are."

"Loved me?" Harper said mockingly, feeling as though he had to be making fun of her.

"Yes. I've always loved you, Angel. I hope you've known that."

"Just like you loved all those beautiful women you're pictured with in magazines and on TV?" Colt had never lied to her before. Why was he lying now?

"I have loved no one but you. You've always been my Little girl. I think my band thinks I'm asexual. They've dangled all types of women and men in front of me. None of them were you." With her mind trying to figure out if what he said meant what she thought it did, Harper allowed him to turn her around to face him.

"Are you trying to tell me you're a virgin, too?" she asked in disbelief. Her eyes locked on his face.

"I've never lied to you, Harper. I won't start now. When we make love, we'll explore how to please each other together."

"I don't know what to say."

"You don't have to say anything. It was my decision. No woman was important enough to break the commitment I felt between us." He stroked a hand through her hair before allowing his eyes to lower and admire her body.

Harper watched his face and saw only hunger. When his gaze returned to link with hers, there was no denying that Colt felt strongly attracted to her. Watching him stroke over the revived erection tenting the towel slung low around his hips, Harper's breath eased audibly from her lips.

His hand cupped her jaw and lifted her chin to kiss her lightly before teasing her, "I'm used to being at least semi-hard when I'm around you, see you on our video calls, when we talk on the phone, or when a random thought of you pops into my head. You give Wilfred a workout."

"Wilfred?"

An image of the battered book Beau had found in the parking lot popped into her head. Even Harper hadn't suggested putting it in the lost and found. They'd known from the title alone what it was about—a romance between a Little girl and her Daddy.

After Beau read it, he passed it to Colt. He'd shared it with the girls. They'd all written their notes and thoughts in the margins, discussing it on paper rather than out loud to avoid others listening. Even then, they'd protected Beau from any hint of scandal. She'd searched for the author's name at the public library, but they didn't have any others written by him.

"You named your—your penis after the man who wrote that book?" she asked, aghast.

"Yes, it was a teenage boy's joke at first. Over time, it seemed to fit. I understood myself a lot better after reading that book about Daddies and Little girls."

She stared at him with her mouth open before asking, "Do all guys do that?"

"Name their cock? Some, probably a lot. I've never asked them. That would really make my band wonder about me." Colt's eyes twinkled as he looked at her. It didn't take long for her to burst into delighted laughter.

"You!"

"Finish getting dressed, Harper. I'll grab my duffle bag. I left it in the living room."

"You were sleeping on the couch," she pointed out.

"You called my name about midnight. I came in to make sure you were okay. I tucked the covers back around you. On my second trip in, I stretched out to make sure you'd fall back to sleep and decided to stay. Are you angry?"

"No," she answered honestly. "I slept very well. I've been worried about the reunion and the fib I told about us. Besides, you slept on top of the covers. It wasn't like you were all over me during the night," she said, trying to be funny.

"Oh, I plan to be all over you, Angel," he promised as he walked out of the room.

His voice drifted back to her. "I'll just wait for you to be completely awake."

That froze Harper in her tracks for a few seconds before she scrambled into jeans and a T-shirt before he returned.

"Want to show me around town today? I feel like a lot has changed since I left," Colt asked a few minutes later. He lounged against the vanity in her bathroom as she put on her makeup, looking totally at ease.

"Of course. I bet you'll find a few things have changed besides Murphy's belonging to Rio now." Harper tried to sound as if having a Nashville superstar watching her put on foundation was normal. Normally, she didn't bother with too many products. The children didn't care what she looked like, and their parents were too rushed trying to get to work to even look at her. When she poked herself in the eye with the mascara wand, he reached for her hand.

"You don't have to put that on for me," he said softly.

"You're used to being around women who have makeup artists flitting around them. The least I can do is put on some makeup," she said as she blotted the tears running from her eyes.

"You are beautiful just as you are. You also have a way more glamorous idea of what my life is like than is true. Let's go get breakfast and we can compare lives. I spend most of my time with my band or alone when we aren't out on tour."

"That still sounds more exciting than being drooled on," she joked. Her face heated and Harper knew she was blushing when his eyebrows quirked up in a silent message. "Drooling is not sexy, Colt Ziegler!"

"It could be," he suggested, turning her away from the mirror and pulling her close. After a quick kiss, he stepped back as if she were temptation incarnate. "Come on, beautiful. I need coffee."

"Coffee isn't good for you."

"I know. I still need some. Is that diner still open on Main Street? The one with the giant biscuits?" Colt asked.

When she nodded, Colt leaned over and picked her up, tossing her over his shoulder. Harper shrieked and grabbed onto his waist to steady herself. "I'm too heavy. Put me down, Colt."

"You're perfect and no." Colt proceeded to tote her effortlessly through the house. He stopped and picked up her phone and his from the charger in the bedroom.

53

Harper looked down at the floor and back up as she bounced against his back, trying not to focus on his butt. *Damn, he'd always had a great butt.*

"A hundred squats a day," he informed her as if reading her mind as he carefully maneuvered his bulk and his cargo out her front door.

"What?" she asked, trying to pretend she didn't have a clue what he was talking about.

"You're really going to pretend you weren't ogling my ass?" he growled after setting her down next to the truck he'd rented for the weekend.

"Um…"

"That's what I thought. You always were a good Little girl. You never lied to me."

"I had a feeling you'd spank me if I did," she pointed out as he opened the door.

"You're right. Here, let me help you. It's a big step," Colt said, boosting her easily up to the passenger seat with an enormous hand on her bottom. He gave her an extra pat before she settled into place. "I will enjoy spanking you."

"You say that like you'll be around to catch me lying. This is just pretend for the weekend, Colt. I'm not expecting you to be my real boyfriend. You'll have to go back to Nashville."

"The only person who thinks this is a ruse is you. I'm done neglecting our relationship. I should have come back a long time ago."

"You've made a lot of people happy with your songs," Harper countered.

"I have. I plan to continue to please my fans, but there are other things more important than music now."

"Me?" she squeaked.

"You." Colt winked at her and stepped back to close the truck door as Harper stared at him.

Could this really be happening?

CHAPTER 8

"*A*re you going to finish that?" Colt eyed the giant cinnamon roll Harper had ordered. He'd already had several bites throughout breakfast. With Colt, Harper had never worried about being judged for her order at a restaurant or how much she ate. His intake always overshadowed even her largest meal. All that bulk Colt had built required a ton of food.

"No way. Eat it for me," she requested, passing the plate over to him.

"Thanks. This reminds me of the cinnamon rolls they used to have in elementary school before all the rules evolved about calories, salt, and sugar. Mrs. Elaine always gave me an extra one because I was a growing boy."

"You definitely were a growing boy," Harper agreed.

"I wonder if she's still alive."

"She seemed so old back then, didn't she? Elaine is in town. She's in her seventies now, so she would have been in her forties when she worked in the schools," Harper shared. "That doesn't seem so old now —to be in your forties."

"It sounds younger every day," Colt answered, popping the last bite of the treat into his mouth.

"Is there anything else I can get for you?" Tina, their sweet waitress who'd taken excellent care of them, asked.

"I think I'm stuffed. Just the check, please," Colt requested with a smile.

"Mr. Ziegler? Are you here for a concert somewhere?" the server asked.

"No concert in Avondale. I'm here visiting my girl," Colt explained.

"Hi." Tina waved awkwardly at Harper. "You're very lucky."

"Hi! I know," Harper said softly.

"There are two lucky people at this table," Colt corrected.

"Is there any way I could get your signature?" Tina asked.

Harper could see several people listening carefully to the conversation. Were all of them going to mob him? She hadn't considered that Colt wouldn't even be able to go out to a meal without running into fans.

"I'm going to be in town so much you'll get sick of me. I'm just an old Avondale Dragon," he answered smoothly as he handed her his credit card.

"I went there, too," Tina rushed to assure him.

When Colt just smiled, Tina hesitated for a minute before running to the credit card machine to run his card. When she returned, Colt signed the slip, adding a healthy tip. He flipped over his copy of the receipt and wrote something before tucking both under his empty plate.

"You ready, Angel?"

"Sure." Harper pushed her chair back to stand and found Colt behind her, gallantly assisting her.

When they exited the diner, he opened the door for her and wrapped his arm around her waist to guide her down the street. Whispers followed them as everyone recognized the Avondale kid who made it big. Harper felt uncomfortable with all those eyes on her. She shifted slightly away from him.

"It's going to be okay, Harper. They're excited to see me now. In a month, they'll be tired of my face," Colt assured her.

"I don't think that's going to happen," Harper said before glimpsing hurricane Miranda aimed at them. "Incoming."

Colt immediately tensed and moved in front of her as he scanned for a threat. Tears prickled in Harper's eyes at the thought that this was his life—always having to be on alert and ready.

She laid a hand on his back and whispered, "It's just Miranda."

"Hi, Colt. Harper," Miranda greeted them with markedly different levels of excitement when saying their names.

"If you need anything special to add an accent to your music videos, I'd love to offer you ten percent off the regular price of anything in my store," Miranda announced, handing him a handmade coupon written on the back of a business card.

"Thanks, Miranda. I'll pass it along to the magicians who work behind the scenes to make me look good." Colt tucked it into his pocket as he guided Harper back into the cozy spot by his side.

"I'll be glad to work with you personally, Colt. Just give those magicians a day off."

"That's not going to happen, Miranda. I've learned to delegate many things to teams I trust," Colt answered.

"Oh, I could take over for them. Save you a few bucks," Miranda suggested.

"Thank you, Miranda, but no. I have a team I trust and they've never given me a reason to replace them. Now, if you'll excuse me, I have a day off to spend with my girl."

"Your girl," Miranda scoffed.

"My girl," he assured her firmly. His stern tone made Harper shiver after witnessing it. Colt rubbed her back to reassure her.

"Come on, Harper. Let's get out of here."

As they walked away, Harper peeked over her shoulder to see Miranda stewing. "I'm going to pay for that," she said with a sigh.

"You take care of her daughter, right? Rumpelstiltskin?"

"No, silly. Cinderella," Harper corrected him with a laugh.

"Oh, yes. How could I get that confused?" he asked with a twinkle in his deep brown eyes.

"You are bad."

"Seriously, though. If Miranda takes Cinderella to a different daycare, will that hurt you financially?" he probed.

"Not at all. It would make life easier for me. I have a waiting list ready to swoop in to take her slot."

"You're just a softy, trying to do something nice for a toddler stuck with Miranda as a mom?" he guessed.

"You always could see through me."

"I could. I'm not going to mess around in your business unless Miranda steps too far over the line and hurts you. I won't stand for that," Colt assured her.

"Colt, I've survived without you for twenty years."

"And I survived without you for the same length of time. I don't know about you, but I'm ready for more. I'd like to see your place if you'll show it to me."

"It's a daycare, Colt. You wouldn't be interested in that."

"You spend most of your time there. I want to see it."

"Then you have to show me your tour bus so I can picture where you are when the band's on the road," she countered.

"Done." Colt picked her up and twirled in a circle, holding her close.

"Hold on to that one tight," a familiar voice called.

Colt skidded to a stop, holding her tight against him. "Mr. Chamberlain?"

"I was hoping to see you, Colt. I see your lady all the time, but I figured I'd have to fight my way through your security forces," the elderly man joked.

"No way. I'll give them your picture so they send you right through," Colt assured him, holding out his hand to shake his former teacher's hand.

Harper watched them greet each other with a happy smile curving her lips. She wondered if everyone else had a favorite teacher who'd had such an impact on them. Crossing her fingers, she hoped so.

"So, are the two of you together now? I knew that was going to happen in the third grade. You've taken your time to claim her, Colt," he teased.

"Oh, we're not..." Harper broke off as Colt interrupted.

"Definitely, we're together. I finally came to my senses about what was important to me," Colt shared.

"I'm glad. She's one of my favorite people in the world. Teachers aren't supposed to have treasured students, but your group left a mark on me. It's been fun to see where you all ended up—a country singing star, the owner of the most coveted daycare in the city, a brilliant scientist, the next president, and a skilled nurse."

"Oh, I don't think..."

Colt interrupted her gently. "We all know you have a special touch with kids."

Turning to his former teacher, Colt added, "And you put us all together, Mr. Chamberlain."

"I'd like to take credit for crafting that first seating chart, but it was totally random. I just put everyone's names on a scrap of paper and tossed them in the air. Your names all landed together," Mr. Chamberlain confessed.

"And you let us stay together," Harper pointed out.

"I might have been a young teacher who didn't know much, but even I recognized that if something wasn't broke, don't fix it," Mr. Chamberlain answered with a laugh. "Now, you were ready to go enjoy your day. Go have some fun! I'm glad to see you, Colt. I'll look forward to running into you frequently when you're in town."

With a wave, their former teacher walked briskly down the street, greeting people as he passed. Obviously, others recognized his impact on their lives and on their children.

"I'm glad I ran into him," Colt said with a grin. "Come on. Daycare first. Then, tour bus."

CHAPTER 9

"$\mathcal{I}$ can't believe you fit the whole band on that tour bus. Does anyone snore in those bunks? Everyone has to hear it," Harper grilled him as they walked back into her apartment in the early afternoon.

"Oh, we have a couple of snorers," Colt confirmed. "I wear ear plugs."

"That's smart. Does anyone…" She stopped before she could finish that question. Harper didn't need to know.

"We decided early on that any sexual exploits would take place somewhere other than the bus. Security is a big reason, but we all wanted a space that was free of groupies," Colt shared.

"So, no one in the group has hooked up?"

"One of the back-up singers is married to our lead guitarist. Everyone else has a family back in their hometown."

"That's a lonely life." Harper frowned at him.

"It is. The band has been together for a long time. The lead guitarist and the drummer are the same people I found to help me record my first song. My plan is to find some land and create a compound for all our families," he told her.

"Wouldn't you get sick of each other?"

"Did you see how small the space is on the tour bus? If everyone had their own house, it would be like living miles apart when we're off the road."

"Hmm. I'll be interested in hearing more about your plans when you get it hammered out," Harper said airily. She doubted he'd ever be able to follow through with the idea.

"Let's talk about you and me," Colt suggested, changing the subject.

"You want to build us a house, too?" she teased.

"I do. But right now, I have other things on my mind."

Colt walked forward to scoop her up in his arms and carry Harper to the oversized leather sectional that filled her family room. Sitting down, he held her close.

"I'd like to talk to you as a Daddy to his Little girl."

"Really? I mean, you're not actually my Daddy," she blurted, feeling her cheeks heat with embarrassment.

"Do you believe that in here?" Cole questioned, pressing a finger against her chest above her heart.

Harper started to shake her head, but his gaze held hers captive. She couldn't lie to him. "I'm too old to have a Daddy," she countered to distract him.

"There is no age requirement to be a Little." He brushed away that argument. "You're not answering my question. When we were teenagers, you believed you were mine. Do you still think you're my Little girl?"

Swallowing hard, Harper hesitated for a minute before whispering, "Yes."

Colt rewarded her with a steamy kiss that made her tangle her fingers in his T-shirt for stability. "Good. I started asking you to the movies when I recognized you were my Little girl."

"That was forever ago."

"It was. I don't want to wait anymore. Our time together has finally arrived." He lifted Harper easily and rearranged her so she was straddling his lap. Colt pulled her flush against his chest.

Harper wiggled and then froze in place at the intimate feel of his body against hers. She looked up at his face. There was no mistaking the desire evoked by her small motion. She could feel his shaft hardening against her. "Oh!"

"Oh, indeed, Little girl."

"Do you want me to call you Daddy?" she whispered, squeezing her thighs together as that daring thought made her wet.

Colt brushed her blonde hair away from her face as he assured her, "When you're ready, I would like nothing more, but you have to feel comfortable calling me Daddy."

"Are you going to make love to me?"

"Soon. When you're ready. First, we play Strip Rules."

"Strip Rules?" she echoed, trying hard to keep her hands from rubbing all over his body.

"I'll take off one piece of clothing when you tell me something you need from your Daddy. And I'll undress you each time I add to our rules as well."

"Really?" Harper stared at him. "So, if I say I need to be spanked when I'm bad, you'll take something off?"

Colt reached one arm over his shoulder and pulled his shirt off. "My turn."

"Wait! I don't really need to be spanked. That's not one of our rules!" she protested with heated cheeks. Why had she said that!

"When you're naughty, definitely, and probably when you're stressed and need relief. A good spanking will erase all the bad stuff from your life."

"And give me a sore bottom!" she protested, staring at his chest and wondering what would happen if she touched him.

Colt placed her hand on his shoulder. "That rule was already on my list. You just said it first. Touch me. You have my permission, Angel."

Before she could process that statement, Harper's hand stroked over his chiseled skin. She'd seen the fitness equipment on the tour bus and knew he spent a lot of the downtime working out. "Colt…"

"Daddy," he suggested. "Second rule, we tell each other the whole truth."

Colt reached for the hem of her shirt and Harper crossed her arms. "Always? Like, no little white lies to make each other feel good?"

"The whole truth. If you don't like my haircut, I need to know so I change it," Colt explained.

That made perfect sense to Harper. She looked around the room, wishing she could pull the blinds. No one could look inside through the secluded back windows. It was just so light. He'd see all her flaws.

Tugging gently at the bottom of her shirt, Colt said, "Little girl, at some point you'll need to be naked. I can't make love to you in this T-shirt."

"You could," she suggested.

"Not going to happen. Haven't you figured out that I love all your curves? I can't wait to caress you. What you're embarrassed by, I'm turned on to see."

"You're in such good shape..."

"If you were all muscles and angles, we'd hurt each other, Harper." He released her shirt to run his hands up her sides and back down. "Hard combined with sweetly padded sounds like an incredible combination."

His hands returned to the bottom of her shirt and pulled upward. This time, she released her arms and lifted them over her head as she repeated *sweetly padded* in her mind. When it cleared her head, Harper watched his face to judge his reaction.

"Damn, Little girl." Colt's hands swept over her, admiring and enjoying every inch of her exposed skin before tracing the swell of her breasts that bulged slightly over the plain cotton bra. "My imagination had you at incredible, but you're way past that. Maybe spectacular?"

"You're making fun of me," she said, crossing her arms over her chest.

"Have I ever said anything to you I didn't mean?"

Harper paused and searched for something as proof to the contrary, but there was nothing. Finally, she admitted, "No."

"Then put your arms down. Little girls don't hide in front of their Daddies."

Slowly, she lowered her arms and watched Colt's face as he studied her curves. His face looked tense. Her nervousness evaporated as Colt reached between them to adjust the erection tenting the heavy material of his jeans.

"Damn," he hissed and drew her forward to exchange a scorching kiss that left them both breathing heavily.

She whispered, "It's my turn, Daddy," to break the sexual tension between them. Harper swallowed hard and gathered her courage.

"I'd like to know that this is a long-term relationship. You're not going to change your mind on a whim."

"I think that's a given. Neither you nor I chose to settle for something less. We've both waited until the time was right," he pointed out, unbuckling his belt and pulling it from his jeans.

The look of the leather in his hands made her heart leap into her throat. Her gaze focused with laser precision as he wrapped it around his fist. Automatically, she tightened her thighs, not processing that in this position, he would know how that act turned her on.

"It looks like we'll have to experiment with different spanking implements," he observed. His words drew her attention away from the leather strap.

"No, Daddy," she protested before quickly adding to distract him, "It's your turn."

"You only think positive thoughts about yourself," he announced. "I want you to look at yourself through my eyes."

"I don't think badly about myself. I'm just realistic," she countered.

"I don't believe that is true. For me, you've always been a mixture of sweet angel and a devilishly tempting body. How would you describe yourself?"

"We need to get you glasses," she observed quickly to avoid arguing with him.

"I have perfect vision. Say one thing nice about yourself," he challenged.

"I'm good with kids. They don't care when they're little if you've never memorized all fifty states."

"And your appearance? What's one thing you like about yourself?"

Seconds ticked by as she tried to come up with something to share.

Finally, she answered, "I have nice lips. The lady at the beauty store complimented me."

"I agree. You have very kissable lips." Colt drew her in and traced the outline of her mouth with soft kisses that made her wish for so much more.

When her lips parted, asking for more, he dipped his tongue inside to taste her. Harper pulled back slightly when she felt his fingers trace along the band of her bra to the back closure.

"Um..." She didn't know what to say.

Colt lifted his hips slightly to press his cock against her soft mound. "Feel my reaction to what I see. I can't fake this, Little girl. I think we've waited too long to waste a minute more. Let me see you, Angel."

Swallowing hard, she pulled the straps down her shoulders for him. He was right. She couldn't let her fear stand in their way. That didn't keep her from holding her breath as he fumbled with the hooks. He really hadn't done this—or at least not often enough to be adept at it.

When the fabric fell away from her full breasts, Colt eased it off and dropped the garment to the couch without a look. With an expression of a man receiving the best present he'd ever seen, his gaze focused on her body as he cupped her large mounds in his hands. "Damn, Harper."

The air rushed back into her lungs, making her breasts rise suddenly. His groan of arousal sent an arrow of desire low into her abdomen and Harper struggled not to rub herself against his hard erection. She shivered as his thumbs, callused from playing the guitar on stage and physical activity, rubbed over her taut nipples. He leaned her back slightly as he bent forward to capture one peak in his lips, tasting it with his tongue as he pulled it into the heat of his mouth. Threading her fingers through his hair, she held him close, torn between being afraid he would stop and what would come next.

Colt lifted his head, and Harper could see the fire in his eyes. She wiggled slightly against him, feeling brave in the face of his obvious desire.

"Temptress," he growled, releasing her breasts to clamp onto her hips, holding her in place. "You may just be the death of me. It's your turn."

Harper stared at him, trying to concentrate. She couldn't think of anything but being half naked on his lap. Shaking her head, she hoped he'd understand how boggled her mind felt.

"It's okay, Harper. This is a lot to think about. Will you promise to tell me if there's something else you'd like us to add?"

Seizing on that suggestion eagerly, she nodded. "I promise."

"Then it's my turn and I have one last rule to add."

She suspected from his tone this one had to be the most important to him. Harper pulled her thoughts together to focus and laced her fingers over his, still gripping her hips. "What is it?"

"Always rely on the trust between us. I'm sorry in advance for what you'll see on social media or rumors that you'll hear. Whatever negative thing crops up, I want you to have confidence that I'm faithful and that I'd never do anything to hurt you. I haven't. I wouldn't. Ever," he promised.

"I'll try my very best," she whispered.

"That's all I can ask for besides your promise to talk to me if something comes up," he requested.

"Okay." She looked down at herself. "Do I need to strip more?"

"I'll take an extra turn for my extra rule." Colt wrapped his arms around her and rose from the couch, lifting them both to their feet.

Running his hands down her arms, Colt drew her hands to the front of his jeans. "Help Daddy, Angel. Show me you want me as much as I crave you."

Her hands trembled as she unfastened the button and grasped the metal tab at the top of his zipper. His shaft pressed urgently against the material. Harper hesitated and looked up to whisper, "I don't want to hurt you."

"Let me help you, Little girl," he suggested. Thrusting one hand between the denim material and his tight boxers, Colt restrained his cock against his body.

Immediately, Harper drew the zipper down. The material parted on its path, allowing her to see his hand cupping his thick shaft. The sight of him touching himself, even so innocently, made her squeeze her thighs together. The racy thought that she could have done that popped into her head.

"I don't know what you just thought, but I want to try that," he suggested with a smirk.

"Don't make fun of me!" she protested, feeling her self-conscious-ness rebounding tenfold. Harper snatched her hands away from his fly.

Colt wrapped his powerful hands around her shoulders and held her in place as she tried to scramble away. "Look at me."

The dominance in his tone drew her gaze to his face. "Have I ever made fun of you? Even in a teasing manner?" Colt demanded.

Harper stared hard at him, trying to think of something she could use to fling into his handsome face. "I... No, I can't think of anything right now," she finally admitted.

"I don't think you will," Colt said softly. He turned back to the couch to grab her T-shirt before sliding it over her head to cover her body. "I'm sorry I pushed you too fast, Little girl. I would never do anything to scare you."

Grateful to be mostly dressed, Harper dropped her chin and stared at his chiseled chest, avoiding his knowing gaze as she battled with tears that threatened to fall. "I'm scared, Colt."

"I know. How important you are to me frightens me, too. I'm willing to go as slow as you need to move forward in our relationship."

Harper threw herself forward and wrapped her arms around his neck. "I don't think I can survive without you as at least a friend. I don't want to screw that up."

He wrapped his arms around her to hug Harper close. "I am always going to be your friend, Harper. But that's not enough for either of us."

Seconds passed before she finally admitted the response screaming in her brain. "No. It's not enough."

Colt squeezed her a bit closer before wrapping up their conversation before she panicked. "We've taken huge steps today. We set up guidelines for our relationship as a Daddy and Little girl."

Shifting one hand between them, he reviewed the items they'd set up, ticking them off on his fingers.

1. Harper will be spanked when naughty.
2. We both promise to tell the truth.
3. This is a long-term relationship.
4. Harper will think positively about herself.
5. We are going to rely on the trust between us.

"I still don't like that first one," she whispered.

"I know. But I think you need the reminder that I care enough about you to correct your behavior rather than walk away. Leaving you would tear my heart out."

"Mine, too," she admitted.

"Okay. I think we need to get out of here. Let's drive around Avondale and you can show me everything that's changed. Maybe we can go for a hike and get away from the city after that. We've got a few hours before the reunion."

"I'm not very athletic," she reminded him.

"A gentle hike," he amended.

"Okay."

That agreement earned her a soft kiss on the top of her head. Without any outward sign of annoyance, Colt tucked his erection back into his jeans.

"Let me help you with this," he said, picking up her bra.

"Oh, I can do it."

"Not happening, Little girl."

Within seconds, he had her redressed and his snug shirt back in place. Taking her hand, he asked, "Ready to play tour guide?"

Harper placed her hand in his. "Thanks for understanding."

"Always, Little girl."

CHAPTER 10

*W*alking back into her apartment a few hours later, Harper felt so much better than she had when they'd departed. She'd enjoyed showing Colt all the changes that had happened in town. He'd been a wonderful companion—kind, considerate, and focused on her.

"That walk was even fun," Harper commented as she toed off her dusty sneakers at the door and watched him do the same.

"It was. Spending time with you is always enjoyable." He stopped and looked at the clock. "We have two hours until the reunion dinner. Just enough time for a shower and a nap."

Harper studied his face. "A nap?"

"Yes. Little girls need a nap."

"I don't take naps."

Colt simply looked back at her.

"You're going to make me take a nap?" she asked incredulously.

"Are you practicing being naughty?"

"I don't want a spanking," she said, sitting quickly on the couch to block his access to her bottom. One look at his powerful body, and the one eyebrow arched quizzically, quickly corrected her thought that she could keep him from punishing her if he desired.

"Shower. Then, nap," he directed, approaching and stretching out a hand for hers.

Slowly, she put her palm against his. "I don't know if I enjoy having a Daddy."

"Now you're really trying to get into trouble."

"Okay, I like having a Daddy. It's what I've always fantasized about. Not just a Daddy—you!" she blurted, unable to conceal anything from him.

"I'm very glad to hear that because I love having you in my life."

He tugged her to the restroom. Colt drew the curtain around the bathtub and started the warm water flowing.

Without a comment, he returned to her side and drew her shirt over her head. While still nervous for him to see her, Harper knew inside that he was as attracted to her as she was to him. She forced herself to stand quietly as he unfastened her pants and drew them down to her feet.

She stepped out of the garment, feeling very daring. *I can do this.*

Without allowing her time to panic, Colt quickly removed her bra, plain cotton panties, and socks. She could feel his gaze devouring her and felt prettier than ever before. Harper shifted her shoulders back to present herself as best she could.

He stroked a hand up her arm and over her shoulder to cup her face. "You are even more beautiful than I ever imagined," Colt complimented, brushing her hair back from her face. He pulled her close and kissed her lightly.

"Jump under the water, Harper. I'll undress and be there soon," he promised.

"I could help you," she offered, feeling her face heat at her eagerness to help him strip.

"I will take you up on that offer soon, Angel."

As he pulled his T-shirt over his head, Harper inched toward the shower curtain. He twirled his shirt and popped her on the bottom when she stood staring over her shoulder at him.

"Ouch!"

"That hurts less than other implements," he warned as his fingers unfastened his belt.

Shooting him a look that should have incinerated him in seconds, Harper stepped into the tub and flicked the shower curtain back into place with what she hoped was a 'I'm doing this only because I want to and not because you told me to' snap. Spotting her razor dangling from the holder, Harper realized she should take advantage of this time alone. She hurriedly shaved her legs, wishing to finish before he could join her. Harper dragged the bright pink device over the last trace of tiny stubble as she heard him drag the curtain back.

Embarrassed, she snapped back into a standing position and met his gaze. Desire ignited in his brown eyes, making her feel sexy. "Oops!"

She scanned down the length of his incredible body. *Guys really do have those V thingies at their hips. Holy crap!*

Harper had seen men naked on the screen and in pictures before—just never within arm's distance and wet. She stared at his cock as it thickened and grew in front of her eyes. Without a conscious thought, she licked her lips as she wondered what he tasted like.

"You are going to be the death of me, Little girl. We're never going to make it to that reunion if you tempt me anymore." Colt turned and ducked his head under the spray of water.

Taking advantage of the moment as he tried to drown himself under the deluge, Harper finished shaving. She grabbed her bath pouf and poured bath wash on it. Keeping her back to him, she quickly washed the front of her body.

The feel of his hard buns touching hers made Harper jump forward. Her feet slipped on the enameled tub and she reached out for something to steady her, feeling her heart race with panic. Warm hands encircled her waist to steady her, pulling her back against his body.

"Whoa, Little girl. Are you trying to give me a heart attack?"

"Sorry. There isn't enough room in here," she suggested, pressing her hands to her chest to calm the racing beat inside.

"There's plenty of room. You're just a tad skittish," Colt suggested.

"It's not like I shower with men regularly. Or ever!" she defended herself.

"I'm okay with that. Hand me that pouf and move your hair. I'll wash your back."

It was easier to follow his instructions. She surrendered the soapy ball and reached up to gather her hair in her hands. Loving Colt's arm wrapped around her waist to keep her safe, Harper savored the long strokes of the soft material along the length of her spine. A girl could get used to this.

Colt stepped out of the way to allow the water to flow over her back and rinse away the soap bubbles. "Anything else left to wash?" he asked in an implied offer of help as he stroked the netting over her bottom.

"No. I'm good," Harper rushed to assure him, and held her hand out.

When he returned the bath pouf, she bravely asked in a rush, "Can I return the favor?"

"You're playing with fire, Angel. My self-control only goes so far."

"I'll just wash your back," she protested, feeling daring.

Slowly, Colt turned around in the shower. He pressed his hands against the tiled wall and dunked his head under the water flow for a few seconds before shaking the water off like a dog.

"Hey! You'll get my hair wet," she protested as she gawked at Colt's backside.

When he glanced over his shoulder at her, she knew she'd been distracted for too long. Quickly, she spread suds over his back, being very careful to wash every hard, muscled inch. When he moaned, she knew he enjoyed her touch as much as she had savored his.

"Go, Angel," he ordered gruffly as he stood up abruptly.

"Okay. You don't have to be mean about it. I was just trying to help," she groused. Even ticked off at him, Harper appreciated his help in stepping out of the tub safely.

The moment the shower curtain flicked back into place, Harper heard him move and then gasp. The steam rising over the top of the railing evaporated. She could feel the chill in the air and knew that

Colt had resorted to another cold shower. Harper clapped a hand over her mouth as she giggled.

Grabbing a towel, she dried off quickly and rushed into the bedroom to struggle into her shapewear before he emerged. A couple minutes later, she heard the water turn off and the rings slide on the shower rod, heralding his exit. Tugging the tight garment up her full thighs, Harper danced as she pulled it into place. The water turned on and she heard him brushing his teeth.

Mumble, mumble, mumble. Colt said something as he cleaned his teeth. The words were so jumbled she couldn't tell what he was saying. "What?"

The mumble repeated a bit louder. She could hear his voice drawing closer as she lifted her smooshed breasts into place. "Oh, gotcha," she improvised to answer him, gambling that it was generic enough to apply to many situations.

Harper smoothed her hands over any small wrinkles as she dashed to the closet to find her favorite of the new dresses from her closet. Forcing herself to slow down and not damage the material, she extricated the hanger from the gorgeous garment and unfastened the zipper as she reminded herself he'd already seen her naked. Somehow, being partially dressed felt more nude than totally bare did.

"Where are you, Angel?" Colt called from the bedroom.

Throwing the fabric over her head, she settled it into place. "I'm putting on my dress."

"Need any help?" he asked, appearing in the opening as the hem settled into place. He stopped as she came into view. Very deliberately, he reached for the light switch and flipped it on.

She blinked in the sudden glare of the fluorescent bulbs above her. Even half blind, Harper could see him scan her body. "Want to zip me up?"

"Damn." Colt walked closer. "Turn around."

Feeling awkward, Harper turned her back to him. She felt his cold hands against her skin and shivered. "You're like an ice cube."

"I thought I was back under control until I saw this dress. You look amazing." His hand released the zipper when it reached her neckline.

75

"Turn around, Angel."

Slowly, Harper rotated in a small circle, trying to be graceful in the small area. She searched his face for a negative reaction, but only saw him smile in delight.

"You look amazing, Harper. I'm going to have to fight off the men with a stick."

"You're too sweet," she murmured, knowing that statement wasn't true. She'd been in Avondale all her life and no one was knocking down her door.

"I'm a lot of things, but sweet isn't one of them," he answered huskily.

"I'm glad you like this dress. It's one of those you bought for me." Feeling a surge of guilt, she added, "I'll be glad to pay you back if you'll give me some time."

"You've already paid me back by letting me camp here." When she opened her mouth to protest, he shook his head. "I enjoy doing things for you. You want me to be happy, right?"

"Yes, but…"

"No buts. Now, I'll get dressed and we'll go."

"I have to put my makeup on," she protested.

"You look perfect now, but I understand." Colt stepped backward out of the closet to allow her to pass, and watched her walk to the door of the bathroom.

When she disappeared from his view, Harper heard a low wolf whistle. She smiled at her image in the mirror. *I love this dress.*

Her phone buzzed and buzzed again and again. Picking up the device, she opened it to find a flood of messages arriving from Colt. *Will you go to dinner with me?*

"Stop, you goof!" she called, grinning at the reminder of their care-free days when Colt worked so hard to take her to the movies.

"That's Daddy goof to you."

Giggling hard, Harper had to wipe the tears of amusement from her eyes before putting on her mascara.

CHAPTER 11

*W*hen her phone rang, she jumped. Looking at the screen, she saw Amber's name appear. Quickly, Harper answered.

"Hello?"

"Harper! Are you heading over to the reunion?" Amber's voice sounded excited and happy.

"We're walking out the door right now."

"Be ready for some questions," Amber warned.

"Just give me a hug instead," Harper whispered, looking over at Colt, who stood by the door.

"Fifteen minutes, Amber. We'll meet you there," Colt called toward the phone.

"I'm putting my shoes on," Amber reassured Harper.

A visual image of the devastatingly handsome gray fox in formal wear popped into Harper's mind, making her blurt, "Tell me he's wearing a suit."

"He's wearing a suit."

"Damn. See you soon." Harper ended the call.

"No lusting after Rio, Little girl," Colt said with a steely look, understanding the conversation without hearing both women talk.

Her cheeks flooded with heat, and Harper knew she was blushing. "Sorry." She allowed herself to scan the image he presented and felt the warmth move lower to settle in her abdomen.

"I'll do as a poor substitute?" he asked with an arched brow, and she guessed her expression revealed her appreciation of his appearance.

"You would never be a stand-in for anyone, Colt." Harper walked forward and lifted her hands to reach around his neck and straighten his shirt collar. When Colt took advantage of her closeness to nuzzle kisses against her neck, she clung to him.

"There are a lot of handsome men in the world. I can appreciate them, but I'm not attracted to them. Since grade school, there's only been one guy I've been interested in—ever."

"That better be me," Colt growled, looping his arms around her waist and pulling her close.

"It's you. Of course, everyone thinks you're doing me a favor by pretending to be my boyfriend for the reunion."

"There's only one person who might believe that, and I think most people stopped believing anything that comes out of her mouth a long time ago."

"Miranda."

"Guess they'll have to change their minds when I settle back in town," he pointed out before changing the subject. "It's time. Let's go, Little girl."

She allowed Colt to guide her to the door. He stopped and picked up her small handbag from the table as they passed. Harper smiled to herself. She loved how Colt took care of her.

On the way to the reunion, Colt chatted about people and places they passed. He'd turned the radio down low, providing a bit of ambience to the trip. Of course, he played the local country western station.

When a familiar tune started, Harper leaned forward to turn it up. "Hey, you're on the radio."

"Ah, that's an old one."

"I like it." Harper listened for a few minutes before singing in harmony with Colt's part. She nudged him and gestured for him to join her.

As he sang, Harper noted that his voice was deeper and richer than it had been straight out of college. Her eyes drifted over his powerful frame as she sang along to the radio, just as she always did when one of Colt's songs played. He'd left town as a teenager. This attractive, powerful man had replaced him.

They were pulling into the parking lot when the last notes died out. Silence filled the cab as Colt parked the car. Pushing a button, he turned off the power and shifted to look at her.

"I miss singing with you, my Angel. We need to do more of that."

"I'd like that, too."

Colt squeezed her knee. "Stay there. I'll come help you out."

As they walked toward the entrance, a familiar voice called, "Wait for us, guys!"

Turning around, Harper smiled at the sight of Maisie and Beau headed their way. "Hey! Good timing."

"I think I saw Rio parking," Beau said as he leaned forward to kiss Harper's hand gallantly.

"They'll have to pass us here. Let's all go in together," Harper suggested.

Harper tried to control her smile as Amber approached, being herded safely out of traffic by Rio, who definitely was wearing a killer suit. She looked over at Colt to focus on his appearance.

"Damn," Colt's voice called across the last few yards as they approached. "I don't know who's prettier—Amber or Rio."

"Amber, of course," Rio corrected him before shaking hands with Colt and Beau as the ladies hugged everyone. "Shall we go in? I have a feeling this group is eagerly anticipated."

"Harper, that dress is gorgeous. It didn't come from Avondale," Amber suggested, scanning her friend's beautiful appearance.

"I might have treated myself to a trip out of town," Harper confessed.

"It's so flattering," Maisie added. "You look curvalicious. Someone can't keep his eyes off you." She nodded Colt's way.

Harper could tell that as soon as they were alone, Amber would have a million questions to ask her. She wished she knew all the answers.

The group moved inside after checking in and claimed a table where they could sit together. Amber, Maisie, and Harper moved close when classmates mobbed the men. After a few brief minutes, Rio extricated himself from the crowd and gathered drinks for everyone.

Armed with a glass of wine, Harper drank in sips. She never drank anything alcoholic, and could tell as good as it was, she'd have to be careful not to overdo it.

"So, we've talked about what we've been doing for the last twenty years. What are everyone's plans for the next five or more?" Amber asked.

"Now that Harper and I are together, we have big decisions to make." He hugged her close as the others looked at them with expressions of hope and concern.

"Together, together?" Maisie asked.

"Together," Colt confirmed.

"Congratulations," Amber said.

"Thank you," Harper answered softly. She crossed her fingers behind her back. *Please don't make me tell our friends that it's all a ruse.*

When the topic of everyone moving back to Avondale arose, Harper held her breath. She'd missed everyone so much. It would be a dream to have everyone back together, even for a small portion of the time. Everyone sounded very positive, except Maisie. Harper had to grin at her staunch resistance to moving back to the town where the residents had judged her harshly based on her family background. Harper could tell they were going to have to work on her to change her mind.

And then Miranda arrived and started flirting with Rio. Harper rolled her eyes, being careful to look at the floor where the catty woman wouldn't notice the movement. Surely even Miranda could see she didn't have a chance with Rio. His eyes were laser-focused on

Amber. With perfect timing, their class president called everyone to order, forcing Miranda to take her seat.

The meal was surprisingly good for something served to a large group. When Rio led Amber onto the dance floor, Harper propped her elbows on the table with her chin on her palms to watch, marveling at the fairytale ending that seemed to be happening for her friend. Rio danced superbly and led Amber across the floor as everyone admired them.

"He's not the only one who can dance," Colt told her softly and stood to extend a hand for hers.

"Oh, Colt. I don't dance," Harper tried to excuse herself.

"That gorgeous dress needs to be shown off," he informed her as he coaxed her into joining him.

Trailing behind Colt, Harper focused on the industrial carpet below her feet so she wouldn't see the looks of her former classmates. They had to be buzzing with gossip about hometown Harper and Colt, the country rockstar.

When he took her into his arms, she held herself stiffly against him. *Don't make a fool of yourself.*

"Relax, Angel. Concentrate on me. They say dancing is like making love—you can tell how well you will be together by dancing with your paramour."

"Really? No pressure here now," she muttered, trying not to fall over her own feet. "I'm used to doing the chicken dance with toddlers."

"I appreciate you distinguishing between dancing with me and your kiddos," he said with twinkling eyes. "I do a pretty mean chicken dance."

Colt flapped his elbows up and down as if he were a rooster boogieing down. When he rocked his head back and forth as if he were going to peck something, Harper burst into laughter and relaxed against his chest.

"That's my girl," he praised her.

The couple swayed to the music. Harper rested her cheek on his chest, listening to his heartbeat. Strong and steady, each thump made her wish to freeze time to stay in his arms.

"Are you ready to get out of here?" Colt asked, rubbing one hand up and down her spine.

"Now? I mean—it's early. You'll miss out on time to talk to everyone."

"I'll talk to our crew soon and everyone else… I don't care if I talk to them or not. I'm not here for my old classmates."

He came to see me. The thought ricocheted inside her brain. No one had ever been more interested in her than everyone else. Quickly, she forced herself to remember he was attending because the group had pinky sworn an oath to make it to this reunion.

"Rio and Beau are handsome, but I don't swing that way, and Amber and Maisie chose their Daddies a long time ago. Just like you belong to me. I'm glad to see our friends but you are why I'm here, Angel."

"You're better than the band. They should send the band away and let you entertain us," a strident voice observed beside them.

Harper turned her head to see Miranda swaying to the music next to them. She did not have a dance partner.

"You don't mind if I cut in, do you, Harper?" Miranda moved to insert herself between Harper and Colt.

Colt did not cooperate. He simply turned Harper so his back faced the interrupting woman. "Melinda, you'll have to find another dance partner. Harper's mine."

"Miranda," the woman corrected him with a glare.

"Excuse us," Colt requested and danced smoothly away from the disagreeable woman.

Harper glanced over her shoulder to see Miranda standing stock still in the middle of the dance floor. What had she thought would happen? If Miranda wasn't already her enemy, she was now.

"I hope she doesn't create a problem for you," Colt said.

"She's already a problem for everyone. If there are any daycare centers left that she hasn't been thrown out of, I've probably lost a toddler. That's okay. I have a waiting list."

"Of course you do. I'd want to be one of your students."

"You might be a bit biased."

"Maybe. I also know how much you care for those kids."

"I do. I missed them on Friday."

"Have you thought about expanding?" he asked.

"I have. I even contacted a property owner to see if he would sell me a small section of the land he has up for sale. Unfortunately, he didn't want to divide the property and I couldn't afford the whole parcel of land."

"Hmm. That was disappointing. It was the perfect location?" he asked.

"The best one ever. But let's not talk about that now. Can we just dance?" Harper asked, leaning back to look directly into his eyes.

"Of course. We dance pretty well together. I'm taking that for a good sign," Colt said, waggling his eyebrows at her suggestively.

"Oh, you!"

A few seconds passed and she couldn't keep from asking. "That's not really true, is it?"

"We'll find out," he said softly and kissed her temple.

CHAPTER 12

*T*aking the keys from her, Colt opened the door to Harper's apartment and ushered her inside. His hand lingered at the small of her back as if he didn't want to lose contact with her. When he hung up her keys on the small rack in the short hallway, she knew he had paid attention to how she did things.

As he turned back to her, Harper surprised even herself by asking, "Can we sit down on the couch?"

"Of course." Colt shrugged out of his suit jacket and threw it over a chair, tugging his tie off as he settled on the sofa.

She waited until they were settled before saying, "I don't want to be your girlfriend, Colt."

"No? What do you want to be?" he asked with a completely neutral expression.

"Your Little girl," she blurted.

"Okay."

"That's it? Okay?"

"That's on my list to discuss before I make love to you."

"You have a list?" she asked, relaxing a bit.

"I do. On my phone." Colt pulled the device out of the interior pocket of his jacket and held it up to his face to open the screen saver.

After pulling up a note, he handed his phone to her. It had bulleted lists of activities that filled the page. Curious, she scrolled down the list and scrolled...and scrolled. Her face heated as she scanned the detailed list under lovemaking.

Looking up at him, she asked, "How long have you been making this list?"

"Since I left you."

"Twenty years ago?" she asked in shock.

"Yes."

She looked back at the list again, this time forcing herself to look at the other categories. "You want to have Thanksgiving with my folks and Christmas with yours?"

"Or vice versa. I'm flexible."

"Colt... This is overwhelming," she confessed.

"I know. I wanted you to know that you've been in my thoughts every day. Our road trips are long. I had a lot of time on my hands to think about our relationship."

"I won't settle for Harper being my girlfriend. She's so much more than that," Harper read.

"I completely believe that. You can't just be my girlfriend."

She nodded and felt herself relax. Look at this list! He had thought of her often. Her eyes landed on one large section—Songs about Harper.

"You wrote all these songs about me?" she whispered.

"Yes. My band is eager to meet you."

She looked at him in disbelief, thinking how disappointed they would be in meeting her.

"Stop that. You are more than any song could ever be."

Colt pulled her onto his lap, controlling her automatic move to shift back onto the couch. "You are more precious than anything else, Angel," he repeated.

"That's a lot of pressure."

"You just have to be yourself. That's what inspired them. My love for you," he said softly as he cupped her face and drew her lips to his.

His soft and sweet kisses beguiled her. Harper wrapped her arms around his neck and threaded her fingers through his thick hair. Instantly, he deepened their exchange, providing her with a taste of the passion he held in control. She could feel his neck muscles tense as he held himself back and knew he didn't want to scare her. Harper touched her tongue to his and heard his low moan of arousal. Confidence flooded into her at the audible sign of his attraction to her. Colt could have had anyone, but he'd waited for her.

Tearing her mouth away from his, she met his gaze and asked, "Will you make love to me now, Colt? We've already waited too long."

A scant millisecond passed before Colt scooped her up in his arms. She clung to him as he carried her to the bedroom. Needing to taste him, she pressed kisses to his neck and jaw. He set her gently on her feet next to the bed.

"This feels like twenty Christmases all wrapped into one. I can't wait to open my present," he told her in a gruff voice as he lowered the tab at the back of her dress. "I love this dress. You'll wear it again for me."

"Okay," she whispered, knowing that this memory infused the fabric to make it her favorite dress.

Harper shivered as the cool air in the room slid over her skin as he lowered the zipper. His hands slid inside to stroke over her back as he pressed kisses to her upturned lips. When he lifted his head, she reached up to lower the bodice. His hands pressed hers against her shoulders.

"My present. I get to unwrap you."

When she nodded, he tugged the material down her arms and over her hips to puddle at her feet. His fingers looped into the stretchy material of her body shaper and eased that off as well. The snugness she had struggled with yielded easily to his strength.

Colt smoothed his fingers over the lines etched in her skin by the restrictive garment. "Never again, Little girl. You don't need to confine your curves."

"But everyone…" she began.

"Not you." He held her gaze until she nodded. "Good girl."

After rewarding her with a fiery kiss that would have made her promise him anything, Colt brushed his immense hands down her sides as he knelt in front of Harper. The rasp of the calluses on his fingertips from playing the guitar made her bite her lower lip in anticipation of what would come next as they slid over her outer thighs and down her calves. He unfastened the ankle strap of her high heels and slid each one off to set them aside.

Rising smoothly to his feet, Colt crushed her to his body and kissed her. His tongue tasted her as his hands held her close. Harper could feel the hard length of his cock pressing thickly against her. She wiggled experimentally and felt his erection jerk in reaction.

"You're going to kill me, Little girl," he growled against her lips. Taking a step back, he lifted Harper into his arms, freeing her feet from the material pooled on the floor. Gently placing her on the soft comforter, Colt stepped back to scoot her clothes to the side with a foot before toeing off his shoes.

Harper propped herself up on one elbow to watch as he unbuttoned his crisp dress shirt. Colt pulled the garment off and threw it to the pile on the floor. Enjoying the sight of his tanned skin, she watched his fingers unbuckle his belt and tug it from the belt loops to discard it with a thud to the floor.

"No!" escaped her lips when he turned away.

"Shh, Little girl. I need to grab some protection from my duffle. I'm not going far." Colt unzipped a pocket in his bag and pulled out a box of condoms. He returned to her side and dropped the box on the bedside table.

Harper scanned the label. "Jumbo pack?" she read.

"We're not leaving this bed for a while."

Staring at him wide-eyed, Harper watched him unzip his pants and roughly dispatch his slacks and boxers. He braced himself on the nightstand to slide off his socks before standing to look over her. Harper stared at the sexy image he presented and tried not to stare at his thick cock.

Surely that would never fit.

"You're wearing too many clothes, Harper. Let me take care of that problem."

Colt laid down on the bed next to her and pulled her close. Cupping her head with one hand, he drew her lips to his. As his mouth seduced her, Harper felt his other hand unfasten each hook on the back of her bra. When he drew the supportive garment away, he continued to kiss her until she squirmed against him.

She froze in place when he leaned back to scan her body. Loving the passion that darkened his eyes, Harper pushed her apprehension away. His hand cupped one breast and lifted it to his lips. Exploring her flesh, Colt pressed butterfly kisses to her skin.

"Mmm," vibrated from his lips when he finally captured her tightly budded tip and sucked it into the heat of his mouth.

That hum made the desire already kindling low in her belly ignite into flames. Harper couldn't focus on one thing as he touched and caressed her. Feeling like she needed to bring him pleasure as well, she reached out to caress him.

"No, Little girl."

Colt captured her hands and pinned them above her head. Holding them in one hand, he turned his attention to her other breast, distracting her from his control. His tongue thrashed over her beaded tip and zings of sensation flew through her.

"I need to touch you," she whispered, trying to free her hands.

"You don't have permission, Little girl."

"Please."

"Not now, Angel. Daddy's holding on to his control by a fine line. I need you to be a good girl."

As much as she wanted to touch him, Harper understood. She also wanted to please him. "Later?" she asked.

"Yes, Little girl. I'll definitely welcome your touch later."

"Okay," she whispered.

"Thank you, Angel. You deserve a reward for being so well behaved."

Colt lowered his lips to the sensitive spot between her breasts. Kissing a line down the center of her body, he swirled his tongue around her belly button, tickling her. Her resulting giggles evaporated when he pressed a knee between her thighs, forcing her to spread her legs.

Pressing her wrists hard into the mattress, Colt asked, "Can you keep your hands here for Daddy or should I get my belt to secure you in this position?"

Her eyes widened at that second choice. The fantasy of being tied into place had ricocheted around her brain a few times. Now, it seemed even more appealing to try with him, but not this first time. "I'll keep my arms above my head, Daddy. Promise."

"Hold on to the headboard," he encouraged, helping her wrap her fingers around the wooden slats. When she was in position, he kissed her and explored down the length of her body once again until he knelt between her thighs. His muscular frame spread her legs widely.

He covered the soft mound between her legs with his immense hand and squeezed her heat lightly. Stroking his fingers down her cleft, Colt explored her body. Harper closed her eyes to concentrate on the sensations, but quickly reopened them to watch him.

Leaning forward, Colt inhaled deeply over her sex. She squirmed in embarrassment and his hand clamped over her thigh, tethering her in place as he looked up. Harper froze. The desire that had shone in his eyes had magnified. Her scent turned him on.

Her breath quickened as he lowered his mouth to her lightly furry mound. She watched him press a kiss to her flesh before running his tongue along the line of her pussy. His hum of pleasure vibrated through her, making her want him to touch her more directly.

"Please, Colt."

"Daddy," he growled his correction, looking up to meet her gaze.

"Daddy? I need you," she whispered.

"Let me help you, Angel."

Pushing her parted thighs wider, Colt made room for his broad shoulders between them. He lowered his mouth to her and licked a path through her delicate folds, stopping to taste her juices in unmistakable delight. "Sweetness."

When his lips descended again to her, Colt searched for those sensitive spots that aroused her the most. The rasp of his soft beard against her inner thighs and intimate spaces made her crazy with desire. Each time she gasped or lifted to press herself against him, he explored, seeking the precise location and touch that brought her the most delight. Tingles gathered between her legs and she shifted restlessly under his attentions. The feel of him tracing her opening with the tip of one finger was the last push she needed.

"Ah!" Harper cried out into the room as pleasure cascaded over her body. She shook underneath him as he inserted one finger and then two to prolong her orgasm.

Harper gasped when Colt scissored them inside her. The slight bite of pain pushed the sensations higher, making her lose the battle to hold part of herself back. When he circled her clitoris with the point of his tongue, she abandoned herself to his lovemaking.

She was almost there again when he rose onto his hands and knees to shift higher over her. Harper could see the moisture glistening on his beard and mouth. She knew those were her juices. He pressed his lips to hers, sharing the flavor, and she forgot where her hands were supposed to be. Exploring the bunched muscles of his shoulders, Harper pressed herself toward him, eager to see what he had planned for her next.

Colt lifted his head. "Tsk, tsk, tsk, Little girl. You are so naughty."

"What?" she whispered, discombobulated. Was she doing something wrong?

"Your hands, Angel."

"Oh!" Harper threw her arms up over her head to get back into position.

After pressing a fiery kiss against the sensitive cord of her neck, Colt reached for the box on the nightstand. Quickly, he unsealed the carton and extracted one packet. "Bad Little girls earn punishments."

"Punishments?" she asked as he carefully tore open the condom and pulled it from the package.

"You'll have to be Daddy's helper now." He handed her the condom and rose to his knees.

When she looked at him, not understanding, Colt drew her hands toward him. Curling up from the bed, she tried to follow his instructions as he coached her through rolling the protection over his shaft. Heat radiated from his body as she touched his cock. Hard, yet soft—a line from a romance novel popped into her mind that he was like velvet-covered steel. Being brave, she explored his body as she completed her task.

"Is that okay?" she asked when it was in place. The sight of his hands moving to make slight adjustments was hot. She reached forward to stroke over his hard chest.

Colt lowered himself to one forearm and kissed her deeply. "I'll go slow, Angel. Back into position."

He captured her hands in his when she raised them again above her head. As much as she wanted to touch him, Harper craved being under his control. Holding her breath as he pressed his pelvis to hers, she felt him guide the broad head of his cock to her opening. When he pushed forward, stretching her tight channel, she tensed. Colt tightened his grip on her fingers and nuzzled against her neck.

"Let's count how many kisses it takes for Daddy to be inside you," he said, pressing a kiss against that nerve-rich site where her shoulder and neck merged.

When she said nothing, he directed, "Aloud, Angel."

"One," she whispered and then gasped as he slid further inside her.

"Two," Harper announced as he kissed that little area behind her ear.

One hand left hers to cup her breast, kneading it softly, and the next kiss landed on her collarbone. When she forgot to say a number, he pinched her nipple and pushed further in as she concentrated on the small tweak of pain.

"Three," she squeaked, feeling the pressure building inside her. "I don't think you're going to fit."

"I'm going to fit."

Colt kissed her lips, dipping inside to taste her. She loved his flavor and responded eagerly for more. When he rocked his hips against her, she widened her thighs a bit more and he eased further inside her. His thick shaft rubbed against a spot inside her that sent shivers through her body. Experimenting, Harper wrapped her legs around his waist.

On the next press forward, Colt's pelvis met hers. He lifted his head to look down at her. "Good girl."

"Four," she announced with a smile. Her fingers tightened on his when Colt glided out and thrust back inside.

She gasped as his shaft rasped over several sensitive spots inside her. "More."

He chuckled before moving over her. Harper loved the feel of their skin pressing against each other. Heat built inside the room as they moved together. She'd worried so much that she wouldn't know what to do. Colt wiped those thoughts out of her mind. He touched her as if she were the most desirable woman on Earth. She reveled in the heat that radiated from his gaze.

When his next thrust ended with a sexy twist of his hips, grinding the root of his cock against her clit, Harper's breath caught in her throat. "There. I need more there," she begged.

Repeating that stroke, he drove the sensations higher and higher inside her. They seemed much more overwhelming because he was there—over her and filling her. The intimacy of her actions with this man etched itself onto her heart. Seconds later, she exploded around him, clenching tightly around the thickness inside her.

Colt froze, buried deep. "Damn, Angel. You feel so good around me." He rotated his hips against her to extend her bliss as he captured her lips in hot kisses.

Harper blinked her eyes open to see him watching her. She tugged her hands free from his hold. "I need to touch you."

"Angel," he replied without answering her implicit request for permission. When he kissed her hard, she went for it, allowing her hands to roam. She squeezed her intimate muscles to distract him from any argument.

"Come one more time with me."

Harper nodded even while doubting she was capable of climaxing again. As he moved, she explored his muscular body, loving the slickness gathering on his skin. Tasting him with a lap of her tongue on his shoulder, Harper reveled at her power when he groaned low in his throat. When his thrusts increased, she felt him slide a hand between their bodies to caress her intimately. The brush of his fingers across her clit sent her skyrocketing toward delight.

"Harper!" he shouted into the room in a deep, guttural voice that appealed to her on a primal level. Colt pinched that small bud above her entrance and Harper tightened her hands on his body as she exploded around him.

When their bodies calmed, Colt rolled onto his side. He took care of the condom quickly before wrapping an arm around her to shift her to lie against his chest. His hands stroked up and down her spine as he pressed frequent kisses to her temple.

Sated and happy, Angel was almost asleep when she mumbled, "How many condoms are in that pack?"

"Not enough. We'll get more, Angel. Now, sleep."

Satisfied by that answer, she tumbled into dreams. Like always, the knight in shining armor that came to sweep her off her feet had dark hair, a lush beard, and a body that rocked.

CHAPTER 13

$\mathcal{M}$onday morning, Harper dragged herself out of bed at the ridiculously early time she did every workday. She tried to move without disturbing Colt's sleep, but he roused the minute she stood up.

"Go shower, Angel. I'll make us some breakfast." His voice, deep with sleep, sounded so sexy she had trouble concentrating on what he'd said.

"Shower, Little girl," he reminded her when she didn't move.

"Oh!"

Harper scurried from the room to turn on the shower and let the water warm as she used the toilet. She could hear Colt rustling with the bedcovers and knew he was making the bed. It felt fantastic to have him there. Stepping into the shower, Harper felt tender from their lovemaking. A smile spread across her lips as she replayed Colt's expert lovemaking. She would have never guessed it was his first time as well.

He wouldn't have told me that to make me believe he hadn't had sex before, would he?

"Hurry up, Angel. I want you to have time to eat something," Colt said, running his hand over the shower curtain.

"Oh! Sorry. Lost in my thoughts."

Peeking out of the shower curtain, she saw Colt standing at the toilet. "Oh! Sorry!" she apologized, flicking the barrier closed again as her face heated. She didn't mean to peep at him peeing. Harper had seen a lot of little boys using the toilet. Colt doing the same thing was totally different.

"You've said, 'Oh, sorry,' too many times, Angel. I think you might be distracted today."

"I wonder why?" she called through the curtain and popped her hand over her mouth at her sassiness.

"Several orgasms seem to have made you spunky, Little girl. Be careful you don't cross the line to disrespectful. Your bottom won't appreciate that," Colt warned.

Eek! "Yes, Daddy."

"Two minutes."

Quickly, Harper cleaned the remnants of their lovemaking from her body. Jumping out, she found Colt waiting with a towel. He gently dried her skin with soft strokes of the terrycloth. When she gasped softly as he dried between her legs, Colt kissed her lightly.

"I'm sorry you're sore. A soak in the tub tonight will make you feel better."

"I don't mind it. It… It makes me remember making love with you," Harper admitted.

Colt hugged her tightly against his body and held her for several long minutes. "I love you, Little girl. I always have."

"I love you, too. I wish I could call in sick today."

"You love your kiddos at daycare. I'm not going away. We'll have plenty of time to spend together. I thought I'd hang out with you today."

"Really?"

"Really. As much as I adore you wrapped only in a towel, I don't want all the parents to see you like this. I've laid out some clothes for you on the bed. Let's get you dressed."

Her mind, whirling at the thought of him going through all her clothes to find something for her to wear, made her embarrassed. He would have seen her raggedy grandma panties and her sizes. Harper allowed him to guide her back to the bed where a T-shirt, jeans, bra, panties, and socks waited for her. Thank goodness he chose things from her closet that fit. She would have hated to explain why she had jeans two sizes smaller and larger.

Picking up the panties, she held the garment out to step into them. His hand closed over hers. "Daddy's job, Angel."

"I need to wear all blue today, Daddy. Could I get a different color shirt?"

"Of course. You choose your favorite and bring it back here."

When she turned with her selection in hand from the closet, Colt had stripped off his gray T-shirt and was pulling on a blue one as well. The muscular grooves of his torso made her fingers itch to trace them. When he caught her staring, Colt beckoned her close.

"Come here, big eyes. Let's get clothes on you." With a few kisses and caresses, Colt dressed her. No one ever cared for Harper. It was always her tending others. She thought she'd feel awkward, but Colt made everything feel right.

"What do you usually eat for breakfast, Little girl?"

"Sunflower butter toast. I eat as I drive."

"That's not safe," he commented with narrowed eyes.

"I'd have to get up earlier to sit and eat," she protested, looking at the clock. She had just enough time to slather some of the thick mixture on a piece of untoasted bread before she'd need to leave. Harper scooted around Colt to dash to the pantry.

Quickly, she made her breakfast as he watched before opening the fridge for her usual brown bag of snacks. "Crap. I forgot to pack my lunch last night." She grabbed a bottle of water before shutting the door with a definite push.

"I'll take care of it and bring you something." Colt picked up his keys and headed for the door, herding her in front of him. "I'll drive you so you can eat."

"You don't have to do this," she protested.

"Yes, I do."

A few seconds later, Harper offered him her topped bread. "Want a taste?"

"Thank you, Angel. That's so sweet. I'll grab something after I let you out to open the daycare."

"Are you going to get fast food? Could I have a large iced coffee?"

"No. I will get you some milk."

"I have that at the daycare," she groused.

"Perfect. Depending on caffeine to fuel your day is not good for your health. I'll need to put you in bed early to make sure you have enough sleep."

"R-Really?" she asked, pulling the word out suggestively.

"Don't worry. I won't forget to budget time to make you squirm. Did you sleep well last night after your bedtime story?"

"I didn't read anything last night."

"No, Daddy told you a bedtime story," Colt jogged her memory.

"Oh! You mean…"

"Exactly what I mean. It was a particularly tasty story," he suggested.

"Daddy!"

Thank goodness it was still dark. Her face flamed with embarrassment as the image of him feasting on her leapt into her head. She popped the last of the bread into her mouth and chewed furiously.

Colt laid a hand over her thigh and squeezed. "I enjoyed all our play last night and plan to exhaust you with pleasure for the rest of time. We've lost too many years together. Now that I've got you, I plan to savor every inch of you. I hope I pleased you?"

She nodded without hesitation and breathed a sigh of relief at seeing the daycare in front of her. Colt pulled into the parking lot and took her designated spot at the end of the parking lot. When she put her hand on the door to open it, he tightened his hold on her leg. She relaxed against the seat back.

Colt slid from the truck and rounded the hood to open her door and lift Harper down to her feet. He kissed her softly before stepping back from the door to let her run up to the entrance. When she peeked over her shoulder, Colt stood leaning against the truck, waiting to see that she got inside safely.

Damn, he looks good.

Harper waved and dashed inside. Within minutes, parents toting sleepy children arrived. She always loved seeing which ones were morning people. Even at a young age, it was very obvious who had instant energy when they woke up and who would want to play late into the evening. With half playing together and half falling back to sleep in the cribs, Harper kept to her regular schedule. Kids always did better with a dependable routine.

Colt arrived with a large bag and waved a suspiciously light-colored cup her way. "I had them make this with half the coffee of a regular iced drink. We'll wean you off caffeine in the mornings."

"Thank you, Daddy," she said gratefully, pouncing on it.

When the door slammed open, making everyone jump and scaring a few of the children, Harper looked up to see her least favorite person. Thank goodness Miranda hadn't been there a few seconds earlier to hear her call Colt Daddy.

"Are you going to pay attention to the kids today or..." Miranda waved a hand at Colt, who immediately bristled.

Harper quickly answered, "Of course, Miranda. Today is a special day. Everyone is wearing blue."

She looked over Cinderella in her mom's arms, distinctively dressed in white and gold. Once again, Miranda hadn't participated in the activities Harper planned. She had some stretchy leggings for kids to wear if their parents had forgotten.

"Hi, Cinderella. Are you ready to play with your friends?"

"Bluh!" The young toddler waved a hand at everyone else who wore the same color as her mom stood her on the floor.

"That's right. Today is blue day. Come on in and I'll find you some blue to wear."

"It's stupid to expect parents to remember things like that," Miranda fussed as she left.

"Cinderella? Would you like to wear something blue?" Harper asked.

When she received the nod of approval, Harper added a pair of blue leggings to Cinderella's outfit. The child looked at herself and patted her leg. "Bluh!"

When Cinderella waddled away to play with the others, Harper rolled her eyes at Colt. She didn't say a word about Cinderella's mother. The toddler would have to draw her own conclusion about her mother in a few years.

* * *

WAVING goodbye to everyone as their parents picked them up, Harper felt full of energy. It had been amazing having help with simple things like cleaning up after lunch or putting shoes on for outside play time. She leaned against Colt at the door.

"Thanks. This was a fun day," Harper told him.

"It was exhausting. You have the energy of four kiddos. And who knew you could create a whole, nutritious meal that everyone could eat that was blue!" Colt tightened his arms around her to hug Harper close.

"And how many songs do you know with the word blue in it? The kids had a blast dancing around," Harper said with a laugh. "I think I've had enough blue for a while. I think the kids got it and had fun."

"I think we all had fun. Come on, Angel. It's time to go home. You can soak in the tub while I make dinner."

"I can…"

"You can soak in the tub while I make dinner," Colt repeated with a glint of 'don't push your Daddy' in his eyes.

"Okay. That sounds nice," she conceded.

Looking out the window as they drove home, Harper smiled at all the couples walking together. When Colt wrapped his hand around her thigh, she leaned back against the seat back and relaxed. It was amazing to have someone in her life. *Please, let this last!*

As if to interrupt her thoughts deliberately, Colt asked, "What punishments do you feel would be most effective?"

"For me?" she squeaked.

"Yes."

"Now? I'm sure I didn't do anything…"

"In general, Angel. What punishments do you feel would help you remember to take care of yourself?"

"A stern talking to would work, I'm sure. I've never really gotten in trouble, so I shouldn't be such a handful," she assured him.

"I think spanking, corner time, and perhaps a loss of privileges or a toy."

"I don't think any of those will be necessary."

"Perfect, we agree that you would learn a lesson from all of those."

Quiet filled the cab as he turned down her street. Colt parked and helped Harper from the high truck seat. As her feet touched the ground, she whispered, "What privileges would I lose?"

"Hmmm," he said, seeming to look. "Things that you would regret, like wearing panties or sleeping in your nightshirt."

"I can't go around without underwear, Colt."

"Daddy," he warned as he escorted her into her apartment. "You can."

"No, I can't!" she said, whirling around to confront him. "You don't get to come in here and make…arbitrary rules."

"There's nothing arbitrary about rules, Little girl. Talk nicely to your Daddy, please."

"And if I don't want to?" she challenged.

"Then we have a problem." He stood quietly in front of her, watching her face.

She decided two could play that game and she stared back, not saying a word. Seconds ticked by and she didn't back down. Harper watched Colt pull his phone from his back pocket and scroll through to select something. In his deep voice, he read:

"I would like my Daddy to be strict. I'm too nice to everyone. Someone needs to make me put myself first."

"Would a Daddy be able to make me feel better about myself? That would be amazing."

"Daddies seem to have a lot of responsibilities. That must be hard on them. I would love my Daddy with all my heart for choosing to take care of me."

"Maybe the most important thing a Daddy and Little can do is talk to each other. I know I can't read minds."

"Do you know who wrote those, Angel?" Colt asked, looking up to meet her eyes.

"I... I did. In our book," she admitted, recognizing those statements she had written so many years ago.

"Have you changed your mind about any of those observations? It's okay if you have. People change. Needs differ," he suggested.

Harper hung her head and remembered trying to come up with even one of those comments in the margins of the book. She'd thought about each one for long periods of time—sometimes days. She'd even practiced writing those words over and over until her handwriting looked immaculate. Adding her thoughts had been important to her.

"How do you have my thoughts?" she asked, trying to deflect the conversation.

"I copied everything you wrote into a notebook. Before I moved away, I typed it up in a Word document. Now, I keep it on my phone. It helps me remember what's important," he shared.

"Maybe I was just rambling."

"I don't think that's true. I think you crafted these from the heart. Has what you desire changed in twenty years, Little girl?"

"No," burst from her lips, shocking her with the vehement denial. Harper looked down at the floor. She tried to figure out what to do—how to make this right. When he walked forward to wrap his arms around her, Harper buried her face against Colt's chest. Clinging to his powerful body, she let his strength steady her.

"It's hard being brave. Did you panic when I suggested punishments, or was it something else?" Colt questioned.

"Punishments," she whispered. He'd brought up the subject of spankings several times.

"I see. Are you scared of getting a spanking or of not wearing panties?"

"Not wearing panties is naughty."

"Is that different than not listening to your Daddy?" he suggested.

After a long pause, she answered, "No. I'm scared of getting a spanking, too."

"There are several kinds of spankings, Little girl: punishments, stress relief, erotic, playful. They each serve a different purpose," Colt shared.

"Erotic?" she whispered. "Like in sex?"

"Usually before sex. You could think of it as foreplay."

"Doesn't it hurt?"

"In a good way. I think you need a demonstration." Colt rubbed her back before setting her slightly away from him. He tugged her blue T-shirt over her head and tossed it over the couch before unfastening her jeans. Dispensing of those quickly as well as her underwear, socks, and shoes, Colt stood up to remove her bra and add it to the growing stack.

"Come lie over my lap, Angel."

"I'm scared."

"Do you trust me, Harper?" he asked. When she nodded, Colt took a seat and patted his lap.

"Will you help me?" she asked, moving to stand beside him.

"Always, Little girl."

Within seconds, he had her stretched over his lap. Colt ran a hand over her bare bottom, caressing her flesh softly. "You are so beautiful, Angel. I am the luckiest man alive to have your trust."

He swatted her lightly, scattering the impact across her bottom and upper thighs. The few that landed right on the seam of her pussy made her gasp. It ignited something inside her. The heat building on her skin made her wiggle on his lap.

"Spread your legs, Angel," he said quietly, interrupting her thoughts.

Freezing at the sound of his voice, Harper hesitated a fraction of a second and felt him deliver a stinging smack on her full bottom. Instantly, she obeyed. Harper knew he could see that she was wet. From the first moment she'd dangled over his hard thighs, she'd felt her juices gathering between her legs. This shouldn't be turning her on... Yet, it did.

"Good girls sometimes ask for spankings, Angel," he told her in that deep, quiet voice as he swatted between her legs. The vibration of that impact flowed through her body. "I'm always glad to pay attention when you need my help."

His hand ceased peppering her bottom to rub over the pink skin before tracing the seam of her pussy. Easing into her pink folds, he explored her reaction. "Mmm, you're very wet, Angel, but not quite wet enough."

Colt lifted his hand to return to landing swats to her full bottom. At infrequent intervals, he returned to explore her intimately. Brushing over her clit, he sent shivers of sensation through Harper before returning to deliver her spanking. He repeated this pattern intermittently. She never knew when he would stop one to begin the other.

Everything blended together, the sting and the thrill. The next time he fluttered his fingers between her legs, Harper's breath caught in her throat. Those captivating sensations hovered just out of her reach. She thought she could gather them in, but he abandoned his caresses just before all the thrilling zings fused together.

"Daddy!" she protested.

This time, the stinging swat of reproach landed directly on her pussy. The wet sound echoed in the quiet space as the vibrations from the impact were the final push she needed.

"Daddy!" she called into the room, clutching at his leg for stability as she felt her body explode into pleasure.

Colt delivered a flurry of light swats, making her squirm as he pushed her climax higher. When his hand stopped and rubbed softly over her skin, Harper sagged over his lap, trying to catch her breath.

"Daddy? Can you hold me?" she asked, needing to be closer.

Instantly, Colt moved to shift her into his arms. He rocked her back and forth as he sang softly to her. Holding onto him, Harper didn't ever want to leave his arms. He knew her so well.

As her mind calmed, she listened to the words he sang. It was from his first big hit, the one that established his ability as a songwriter and performer. Sung only by him without any instruments or backup singers, the words resonated inside her.

What happens when the time isn't right? When love comes too soon or too late? Remember how it feels, shimmering outside your reach. Use that to fuel you when it reappears. Pay attention, it's time to fight.

"Did you write that about us?" she asked.

"I did. I knew if I had another chance to be your Daddy, I would sacrifice everything to take care of you."

"Everything?"

"Yes, Angel. So, we need to figure this out. This time I will fight for us."

CHAPTER 14

*A*s Harper disinfected the toys in the play area at the end of her workday on Tuesday, she studied the handsome man hard at work putting together another toy bin that she'd never had the time to construct. He'd spent most of the day with her again in her daycare. Colt's presence in her life felt easy and right.

"How do we do this, Colt?" she asked.

"Being a Little and a Daddy?" he asked, looking up from the directions.

"Yes. And merging it together with our real lives."

"Being a Little and a Daddy is real life, Harper," he reminded her.

"I know, but…"

"How do we operate in a world that might not understand?" he probed.

"Exactly!" She smiled at him, happy that he understood. Colt always seemed to get her.

"I have something to show you. Tonight might be the perfect time. It's still light outside. Will you come with me?"

"Yes. Let's put that in the storeroom until you can finish it."

"I'll put it in the truck bed and finish it at home," he decided. "It will get in your way tomorrow."

She wanted to protest that he needed some time off but Harper loved that Colt called her small apartment home. He immediately scooped up all the small parts and tucked them with the directions into the plastic pouch they'd come in. "Open the door for me, Angel, and grab your things," he directed as he stood and lifted the almost finished project in his arms. In two trips, he had everything loaded in his vehicle.

Soon, they headed to the mystery destination. When they reached the road heading for the old high school make-out spot, Harper laughed. "There are too many lights down there now. Kids have another place to hide from their parents."

"You better not know where that is," he said with a glower that made her giggle as he turned off the road onto the dirt.

"This is private property, Colt. I don't think the new owner would like people driving over his land," Harper warned, looking around nervously.

"I don't think they'll mind us being here. I have permission."

"Really? Well, I guess it's okay then."

Harper sat quietly until Colt parked and came around to open her door. When he helped her out, she walked to the very spot she'd envisioned for her beautiful daycare. "When this land came for sale, I asked if I could buy this small section. The sellers wouldn't divide the property. It would have been an ideal spot to build a new business."

She looked again at the prime location on the main road that connected Avondale to the next bigger town. So many people drove this road to get to their jobs there. She shrugged, knowing the cost for only a small section would have been too much.

Harper turned to see Colt watching her. "Sorry. Just lost in coulda, shoulda, wouldas. Why did you bring me out here? What did you want to show me?"

"Would you like to ask the new owner if he'd sell you a small section for your business?" he asked.

"I don't even know who that is, Colt," she answered hopelessly, wondering why he was asking.

"Me."

"You? You bought this land?" Harper looked at him in shock.

"I needed a place to build a complex for the band to record here. This seemed like the perfect spot. I didn't know until after the sale was complete that you had inquired about buying the front section. I've had an architect designing plans for us."

"What?"

"I know this came out of left field, Angel. I would love to have you be able to roll out of bed a few minutes later because your daycare is a walk away from our house."

"You want us to have a house? You're really going to move here?"

"I won't be separated from you again, Little girl. I can do almost everything here. I'll still have to travel and tour from time to time, but staying here with you will be my home base."

"I don't even know what to say." A slow tear slid down her cheek.

"Angel," he said, closing the distance between them to wrap his arms around her. "That better be a happy tear."

"I can't believe this... This is really happening," she stammered.

"I want to hold you in my arms every night and feel your heartbeat next to mine. I want to wash your back and make you dinner at night. Most of all, I don't want to miss another second of your life."

"I want to be with you, too."

"Then here's the start of our new life together." Colt gestured across the open land.

She stood wrapped in his arms, looking out over the wide space around them. A car honked hello from the road. Harper tried to shift away from Colt, but he held her firmly in place as he waved.

"Colt, maybe this isn't meant to be. I'm not really a good match for you. I could try to lose weight, but I always gain it back, and I'm miserable eating broccoli for breakfast, lunch, and dinner."

He pushed her back to arm's length to look directly into her eyes. "Where did that come from, Little girl? Have I ever given you the impression that I thought you needed to change in any way?"

"No. Of course not. You're too nice to do that."

"Did my reaction to your nude body make you think you were not attractive to me?"

"Colt!" She looked around, scandalized, to make sure no one was near.

"Being around you is a constant struggle not to bust my zipper open, Angel. I waited years to make love to you because I didn't want anyone other than you. Your beauty inside and out draws me to you."

"Maybe that's just because you haven't had sex with anyone else? You know, you don't have anyone to compare me to," she suggested, looking down at her sneakers.

"Look at me."

She hesitated, waiting to see what he would say next, but Colt stayed silent. After several long seconds, she peeked up at him. *Crap! He's mad.* His gaze trapped hers.

"Making love means more to me than simply getting off, Harper. I can do that on my own."

She felt her cheeks heat when a visual image of Colt taking care of his needs with his hands flashed through her mind.

"Merging my body with the one person who I knew belonged to me was more attractive than dabbling with a million women who wanted me for my sports prowess back in high school or for my current fame and money," he told her bluntly. "They weren't you."

"I didn't want anyone else, either," she whispered. "I'm sorry to bring it up again. It's a struggle to believe that this is happening." Harper waved a hand between herself and Colt.

Stepping close to her, Colt cupped her face with his hands. "I will reassure you until I die that you are the one for me. I don't want to change or alter you. I want your sweet mind, your luscious body, and the Little girl inside you."

"Okay. I may need you to do that," she admitted. Her mind struggled to adjust to the idea that Colt wanted her—really.

She looked around the beautiful space that he had purchased to be close to her. No one spent that kind of money to move to Avondale unless there was an actual reason to be there. Another worry popped into her mind.

"Would you help me figure out what I can afford to build here? I'd like to expand—have at least one more person working with me," she asked hesitantly.

"We'll work together to build something that is perfect for what you want today and in the future. You might wish to grow further," he replied.

"I don't want to get too big," she assured him.

"I think you want to still be able to interact with each child."

"Definitely, yes!"

"I'll take you with me to the architect for my next visit. We'll sketch out something before we go to show him what you need."

"You already have an architect?"

"I do. Now, let's go celebrate with dinner out. What's your favorite restaurant? Murphy's?" he asked.

"I go there all the time. This feels like a big celebration. Could we go to the Italian restaurant on the square, Salvador's?"

"That's still there?"

"It is. His grandma isn't there making the homemade Italian bread-sticks anymore, but his daughter works there. Hers are almost as good," Harper assured him.

"Let's go. Want to take a picture first?" he asked, pulling his phone from his pocket. "Our first time together at our new home and your new place."

She nodded quickly. Harper wanted a picture to remember this moment—she wanted to remember all the moments. Smiling happily, she cuddled against Colt's broad chest.

"Great picture," he celebrated, turning the phone so she could see it as well.

Harper stared at the screen. She looked beautiful. How had he made her look like that? Watching as he forwarded the shot to her phone, Harper knew that Colt brought out the best in her. She was so lucky to have him.

CHAPTER 15

"Here, Angel. I got you this to help remind you to give yourself a break and that I love you." He handed her a large gift bag with tissue blooming from the top.

"I didn't get you anything."

"I didn't get a present for you to get something in return, Little girl. Daddies are supposed to reward their Little girls when they're good."

"Oh. Okay." Harper had enjoyed being good. It had been almost a week since Colt had taken her to see the land. A new daycare had filled her dreams. Even an outbreak of the flu hadn't brought her down from her high.

"Can I open it now?"

"I'd like that," he encouraged with a smile.

Quickly, Harper ripped the tissue paper up and let it drift down to the floor as she peered down into the bag. Carefully, she scooped the stuffie up in her arms and hugged him, knowing instantly that he was indeed a boy.

"What is he?"

"I had to look at the tag, too. He's a wombat. I think he's quite handsome," Colt suggested.

"A wombat. I'm going to research about him. I can't wait to know all about him. Hmmm. You need a name." Harper held the adorable plump stuffie away from her as she pondered that question.

"Wally? No, that's not quite right."

"You could think about it for a while. I think your new friend would be okay with waiting for you to choose," Colt assured her.

"No, he knows." Harper lifted the wombat to her ear and listened carefully. "Of course. That's an amazing name."

Cuddling the stuffie back against her, she announced, "Wombles."

"That is a very cute name. I like it." Grinning, he pulled her close to hug both of them. "I love you, Little girl."

"And Wombles?"

"And, of course, Wombles."

Colt guided Harper over to the couch and sat down to pull her onto his lap. Over the last few days, she was getting more comfortable about not risking crushing his thighs. Leaning against Colt's broad chest, she explored Wombles' cute face and fur. He was the softest.

"Angel, I don't want to leave tomorrow."

He sounded so sad. Harper threw her arms around his neck and hugged him close. "I'm sad, too. But it will be a quick trip, right?"

"As fast as I can make it. Probably a week. I'll call you every day. I'll make some changes to my schedule in the future to limit time away, but I'll always have out-of-town obligations, Little girl."

"It's okay, Daddy. I'll have a lot here to keep me busy until you get back."

"Really? What are you doing?" he said with narrowed eyes.

"Just work and research floor plans for daycares. I'm sure there are a ton of ideas out there I haven't thought about."

"That's a good idea. I'll ask the architect to research best practices as well."

"Thank you. I can't wait until they build everything and we're moved in."

"Neither can I. I bought me a present, too," he told her. "Go look in the night table on my side."

"Really?" She jumped off his lap to run to the bedroom. Harper loved that he had a side of her bed reserved. She set Wombles on the bed to watch.

Opening the drawer, she saw a collection of condoms that they had diligently worked on eliminating. A vivid pink cylinder caught her eye. That was new. Picking it up, she felt her cheeks heat and knew they were turning as bright as the device in her hand. Slowly, she turned to see him standing in the doorway.

"You are only to play with that when Daddy's with you or on the phone."

She nodded without hesitation and started to put it back.

"Turn it on, Angel. The control is on the base."

"Daddy, that's embarrassing," she pleaded for him to understand.

"No secrets between Daddy and his Little girl, remember?"

"I know," she whispered.

Fumbling, she almost dropped the vibrator as she turned it around to find the button on the bottom. Harper pushed it once and felt the rumble begin. "Nice. I'll just turn it off now." She pushed the center again, expecting it to fall quiet in her grip. Instead, the vibration increased.

"Whoa!"

"Try again," he directed.

As soon as she pressed it, Harper almost dropped it. The louder hum filled the air as it hit turbo drive. "No. That's never happening."

"Oh, it's happening. And you'll love it," he promised.

She shook her head vigorously and debated whether it was safe to press it again. Swallowing hard, she pushed the button again. Silence fell like a cloak over the room. Slowly, she looked up to meet Colt's dancing eyes. "You need to stand in the naughty corner."

"Only if you're there with me, Little girl."

To her astonishment, she found herself nodding. Her Daddy was a bad influence. Or was that a good one? Harper watched him walk forward. He picked Wombles off the bed and pet him softly.

"Time for you to take a nap, sweet guy." He set the wombat on the dresser, facing the wall, before walking to Harper. "I think you need a nap, too, Angel."

She swallowed hard as he unfastened her jeans and drew the heavy fabric and her panties over her hips to cascade to the floor. He scooped her up and carried her to the bed. Dropping her a few inches to bounce on the bed, he scooped up the vibrator when she dropped it to the comforter in surprise.

"Oh, no, Little girl. You need to treat your presents better." He tapped it lightly on his palm before slowly turning it around to press the button. "I think we'll start with level one."

"Start?" she echoed, her gaze glued to the device.

"Yes, Angel. We'll have to try all the speeds to make sure it works."

"Daddy?" she squeaked.

"I'm right here." Colt reached over his shoulder with one hand to grab a fistful of his T-shirt and yank it over his head.

Harper scanned his muscles, feeling that same thrill she always did at the sight of his chiseled body. Colt had found a gym nearby and ran daily. When she'd offered hesitantly to join as well, he'd assured her he'd love to have her with him, but only if she enjoyed working out. When she confessed she hated sweating, he'd taken a couple of hours in the afternoons to go while she was working. She definitely enjoyed the results.

I should be helping, Harper reminded herself, pulling her thoughts back together instead of drooling. Grabbing the bottom of her T-shirt, she tugged it upward, only to stop at his sudden stern look. *Daddy's job.*

After toeing off his boots, Colt crawled onto the bed to straddle her thighs. She could feel his heat radiating to her core. Squeezing her thighs together, Harper held her breath, waiting to see what would come next. Colt was an imaginative lover. He'd quickly taught her that nothing was off limits between them and that he had a cunning imagination.

She watched him start the vibrator. He stroked it along the cord of her sensitive neck, making her shiver, before drawing a line over her shirt, down the center of her chest, and stopping between her breasts. Her gaze flew from the device to his face when he paused there.

With a wolfish grin, he drew a path that circled around her right breast, growing ever smaller until it touched her nipple. Harper bit her lip trying not to moan as the sensation and anticipation built.

"Let me hear your sounds, Little girl," he reprimanded her as he moved the wand over to repeat the process on the other side. This time, she didn't try to curtail her whimpers as he teased her nipple.

The breath gusted into her lungs as he traced a line over her stomach to the mound of her pussy. "When Daddy's gone, I might ask you to grab this vibrator, Little girl."

"While we're on the phone?" she asked, shocked.

"Yes, Angel. I'll tell you exactly what to do. Let's practice. You take this," he instructed, lifting it from her skin and handing her the base.

Harper gingerly accepted it and looked up at him helplessly. "What do I do?"

"Draw a line down your lips."

Slowly, Harper moved the tip along the seam of her pussy, trying not to wiggle. His weight tethered her in place and held her legs together. It slipped in the juices building between her legs. She peeked up at him to see a look of absolute passion on his face. Daringly, she lifted the vibrator from her skin and carried it to her mouth to lick the slickness away.

"You are killing me, Harper."

When she lowered the pink wand back to her nether area, she brazenly brushed it over the tightly stretched denim of his fly. His hand clamped over hers. Holding it and her fingers pressed against him, Colt groaned deeply. Seconds later, he lifted the device from his erection and scooted over to sit sideways on the side of the bed.

As he ripped open the buttons of his jeans, he ordered, "Spread your legs."

Eagerly, she followed his instructions as he pulled his cock from his pants to stroke it roughly from root to tip as his gaze roamed over her body. The heat burning in his eyes made her imagine she could feel it touching her. The vibration in her hand drew her away from her thoughts.

"Run the vibrator between your lips, Angel. Touch yourself how you'd like to feel me touch you," he growled as he slowly pulled the thick shaft in his hand.

Feeling self-conscious but fascinated by him touching his cock, Harper spread her legs. Thrilled by his low groan of arousal, she moved them wider.

"Wider," he growled and she bent her knees to the sides, exposing herself fully to his view.

Bravely, she experimented with the vibrator. The buzz spread across her body as she moved the wand through her pink folds. Harper traced her opening and hesitated before dipping it slightly inside.

"Damn, Angel. You're killing me," he encouraged.

"Sorry, Daddy," she whispered, trying to keep the corners of her mouth from turning up.

"Do it—slowly."

Harper took a breath and pressed the wand into her wet pussy. Her eyes closed as the vibrations filled her. She could feel it echoing through her. "Ahh!" Holding it deep, she pushed it around in a small circle, hitting all the spots that having sex with Colt had introduced her to so well.

Slowly, she pulled it out and peeked at him as she played with the tip over her entrance and daringly to her clit. Colt's fingers wrapped around his cock as he stared at her. His gaze burned hot with desire. As she watched, he reached toward her, trailing his fingers down her inner thigh to brush the vibrator out of the way. He pressed two fingers into her wetness. As he lifted those fingers to his mouth, Harper set the vibrator to the side and jerked her shirt over her head.

"Damn, Angel," he cursed, rising from the bed to shed his clothes. Grabbing a condom, he ripped it open and rolled it on as she unhooked her bra and tossed it off the bed.

"You are such a bad girl," he whispered as he climbed onto the bed, caging her under him as he supported himself on his hands and knees.

"Maybe I need a punishment?" she teased.

"Oh, I'm going to dole out a reprimand you'll never forget."

After tugging the pillow from under her head, he moved backward to lift her hips and slide it under her bottom. Once back in place over her, Colt allowed himself to taste her breasts. Tracing the sensitive underside with his lips and tongue, he distracted her from movement as he located the discarded pink wand and moved it between them. Reigniting the buzz, he pressed it to her clit.

Her body arched under him, trying to evade the almost too much sensation. She reached for his shoulders to push him away when his pelvis moved forward to glide into her in one smooth thrust. Filled and buzzing, she exploded into a massive orgasm that rocked her body.

"Daddy!" she shouted into the room. Clinging to his powerful shoulders, she tried to steady herself as sensations buffeted her body.

"Hold on, Angel."

Their lovemaking was wild and wicked. Holding onto him and caressing everything she could touch, Harper pushed any shyness from her brain. This was Colt. His body called to her, and she responded with all her heart. Each stroke built the fire between them as he surged into her.

Exploding into a million pieces, she cried her pleasure into the room once again. Colt's fingers tightened on her hips as his thrusts increased. With one final thrust, he buried himself deep into her warmth. "Mine!"

When he lowered himself to the mattress next to her, Colt dealt with the condom before pulling her close. He kissed her deeply. "Get ready for phone sex. I'll never forget the sight of you playing with yourself. So damn captivating."

"You swear too much, Daddy."

"I'm sure you deserve punishment for that, too, Little girl. Some-how, you seem to make me forget my manners."

"I didn't hear anything," she blurted, trying to get herself out of trouble.

"Give me a kiss, Angel. That will give me the courage to survive your temptation."

After planting a superb one on his lips, Harper settled against his chest. Her gaze ran over Wombles, lying with his back to them. Thank goodness her Daddy had protected his innocent eyes from their display. Poor stuffie would have been scandalized.

CHAPTER 16

She missed him so much. Harper cleaned the empty childcare center after the last parent had picked up their child. Colt had been gone for over a week and she felt like her heart was shriveling a bit more every hour he was gone. She'd even brought Wombles to work today to keep her company.

Needing to distract herself, Harper stopped at Murphy's on the way home for dinner. Maybe being around other adults would make this hole inside her feel better. She tucked Wombles deeper into the tote so she could carry him in her purse without anyone seeing him.

"Traffic's horrible today, Wombles. Murphy's must be packed."

As she turned the last corner, she saw flashing lights on what seemed like a hundred ambulances and police cars. Unable to pull into the parking lot, she drove past and parked in the lot of the apartment complex next door. Grabbing her keys and the tote bag, Harper ran to the crowd gathered around the barricade the police had established.

"What's going on?" she asked the woman next to her who she knew vaguely from running into around town.

"Someone pulled a gun inside Murphy's. They hurt a few people."

"Oh, no! Do you know who?"

"No. But if it hadn't been for that silver fox bartender, he would have hurt more people. Rio saved the day from what I hear."

"Rio? Is he okay?" Harper gasped.

"That's Mr. Hotness. Look!" The woman pointed as they rolled a distinctive man out on a gurney and the crowd erupted into applause.

Harper waved frantically at him, calling his name, but Rio didn't see her. He was obviously headed to the hospital. Today was Amber's first day in the ER. There was no way she hadn't heard that he was coming in.

Shouldering her way back out of the crowd, Harper said a quick prayer that Rio was okay as she hurried back to her car. Once in the car, she dug her phone from her bag and dialed Amber. It went directly to voicemail, so she knew her friend's cell was off. Harper left a message asking Amber to let her know if she and Rio were okay.

Her next call went to her Daddy. He'd want to know what was going on. It rang over and over before disconnecting. Frowning at the phone, she tried again. This time, it connected on the fourth ring.

"Harper, huh? That sounds like a desperate groupie name. Colt is busy—and naked. Stop calling." With a drunk-sounding giggle, the young woman disconnected the phone.

Horrified, Harper tried to figure out what had just happened. Who had that been? She hadn't called the wrong number. That woman had mentioned Colt. She'd obviously reached his phone.

Dropping the phone to the seat as her mind whirled a million miles, she grabbed blindly for Wombles and pulled him to her chest. "What is going on? She sounded like she was in her twenties. And she was drunk!"

An image formed in her mind of a flashy twenty-something. She was everything Harper was not—willowy, athletic, and gorgeous. "She probably can sing in front of a crowd without wanting to throw up."

Tears filled her eyes, clouding her vision, but not obscuring the picture in her mind of Colt wrapped in someone else's arms. A honk nearby brought her head up, and she looked through the windshield to see the ambulances had all left the area. A few scattered police cars blocked the parking lot, but it appeared the emergency had resolved.

"Let's get home, Wombles."

Taking a circuitous route home avoided the traffic that had built up. When she pulled into the parking lot, Harper dropped her forehead against the steering wheel. It took a minute to gather the strength to drag herself into the apartment.

Inside, everywhere she looked she saw Colt: lounging on her sofa in a pair of ragged gym shorts, joking in the kitchen as he made their lunches for the next day, leaning against the bedroom door with that unmistakable hunger igniting his deep brown eyes. She walked in and dropped her keys and phone on the table before sitting in her grandma's rocking chair. Harper didn't remember him ever settling there.

"Oh, Wombles. What am I going to do?"

Minutes passed as she rocked, trying to reassure herself that everything was okay. She must have misunderstood. Could she have misunderstood?

Her phone buzzed, and she jumped up to run over to the device. A text message stood out on the screen: *Sorry, Harper. I'm booked this evening with a meet and greet. I'll have to talk to you tomorrow. Forgive me?*

"A meet and greet? Is that what they're calling sex now, Wombles?" Harper spat out, feeling the hurt flash into anger. Picking up the device, she turned it off and plugged it in. No one really needed to get in touch with her. *How sad is that?* No one would worry that she was okay. Being alone had never felt so lonely.

By habit, she walked to the refrigerator and looked for something to eat for dinner. At the sight of food, her stomach flip-flopped. Harper stepped back and closed the door with a decisive snap. For once in her life, she didn't have any desire to eat.

Carrying Wombles into the bedroom, she sat him on the bed as she stripped off her clothes, finding sticky handprints and a Cheerio stuck to the back of one leg of her jeans. Dropping the latter in the trash with a sigh, Harper questioned the life purpose she'd always known she was supposed to do. After stepping into the warm spray of the shower, she dunked her head under the water and tried to quiet her thoughts.

Without opening her eyes, she searched blindly for the bottle of body wash. Harper poured some into her hand and slathered it quickly over her skin. Bursting into tears, she inhaled the spicy soap Colt had purchased to keep from smelling like the roses she preferred. Unable to resist, she spread it over her face to savor the scent.

Damn you, Colt.

Harper never cursed, but stealing his favorite swear word seemed appropriate. Why had he screwed with her heart? She would never have pursued him. A daycare teacher after a rich and famous Nashville country star? That only worked in sappy TV movies and the tattered romance novels she hid under her bed.

She watched the thick lather circle around the drain before slipping away. Scrubbing the tears from her face, Harper flicked the water off and stepped out to towel her skin roughly. After drying her hair with the other towel on the rack, she threaded her nightshirt over her head and turned off the lights.

It took the last of her energy to crawl under the covers and cuddle Wombles. With her nose buried in his soft fur, Harper tried to understand what had happened. Had she missed clues? He'd been so good at pretending.

"I should have known, Wombles. Prince Charming isn't interested in a stupid girl from a backwater town."

That amazing corner section of the land he supposedly bought popped into her mind. Her heart broke a bit more. Harper knew she would have been better off if he'd never come to town to show her what she was missing. She'd been happy treasuring her friends, even if she only got to see them on the screen. He hadn't needed to come pretend to want her in his life.

Why?

Finally tumbling into sleep on her tearstained pillowcase, Harper dreamed of the happily ever after she thought she'd found. When she woke on Colt's side of the bed, she blinked at the sight of the time. She was so late.

Throwing on clothes and shoes, Harper grabbed her keys and phone as she dashed out the door. She drove like a maniac to the daycare, finding several parents parked at the entrance. Quickly, she ran in the side door with her heart beating so loud she could hear it as she turned on the lights to welcome everyone fifteen minutes later than usual.

Apologies tumbled from her lips after opening the door. Everyone was very forgiving of her slight tardiness, except for Miranda. The unpleasant woman scanned Harper from her unbrushed hair and red eyes to her mismatched clothing and the flip-flops she wore.

"If you want to have sex in the morning, wake up earlier. We're all working and need to drop off our kids on time," Miranda rebuked.

"I've apologized for being late," Harper said, straightening her shoulders to look directly into Miranda's eyes. She squelched her first impulse to share that Colt was out of town, so she hadn't been screwing around.

"Hmph." Miranda set Cinderella down on the flooring and kissed the top of her daughter's dark hair. "Go play, sweetie. Mamma will see you later."

Eager to play with her friends, the small child rushed to the pile of toys in the center of the room without a look back. Miranda paused to look at Harper before turning without a word to leave.

With arrivals continuing through the morning, Harper rushed around the space, doing the preparations for that day's agenda. She would have had all that set up if she'd arrived on time. Thank goodness the kids were cheerful and flexible that morning. They tolerated her change in their usual routine with a sparkle in their eyes for a mix-up day. She'd have to do this again from time to time for them.

After lunch, a cry of anger and one of discomfort made Harper focus on a small group of three. Kneeling next to them, she scooped up a pile of blocks and set them out of arm's reach. Soothing the annoyance of one who wanted to keep playing and Cinderella, who had a faint red mark on her arm from a flying toy, she scooped up the instigator. He was burning up with fever. Holding him close, Harper rose and rocked the little boy as she rushed to her phone.

Harper fumbled with the phone, finally pushing the right buttons to start it. Messages bombarded her phone screen, notifying her she'd missed several contacts. She ignored everything as she navigated to the parents' names and called the father. As the phone connected, she grabbed the forehead thermometer and held it in place.

"Yes."

"Mr. Erickson. This is Harper. Thomas is running a fever. You will need to come pick him up."

"He was fine this morning."

Harper heard rustling and knew he was gathering his things to leave the office. "It's come on very suddenly. He was fine thirty minutes ago. Now, he's running a fever of one hundred and two."

"That's not good. I'll call the doctor on my way. Thank you, Harper, for calling."

The parents of two children had already appeared to take their sick child home when Cinderella was the next to fall ill. Dreading the phone call, Harper selected the number from her directory—Miranda.

"Miranda, this is Harper. Cinderella is ill and needs to be picked up."

"How sick is she?"

Shaking her head at the first adult who'd asked that question to wiggle out of picking their child up early, Harper strove for a firm tone. "Cinderella cannot remain at daycare, Miranda. She has a fever of a hundred and one."

"That silly rule. Maybe the thermometer isn't working. Try it again."

"Miranda, come pick up your child."

"Fine. I'll be there within the hour."

"Thirty minutes, Miranda."

Harper stared at the silent phone, shaking her head. The woman had disconnected in a fit of anger.

Settling Cinderella in an isolated crib, Harper covered her with a soft blanket. She stopped to wash her hands and grab the disinfectant wipes. Harper sat on the floor with the remaining healthy children.

"Time for music. Are you ready to sing?"

Yeses filled the air.

Harper led everyone in a series of fun songs as she carefully wiped down all the common spaces to control whatever was spreading through the daycare. By the end of the fourth song, the door opened and Miranda entered. A hush fell over the toddlers. Even they could sense it wasn't smart to capture the attention of hurricane Miranda.

"Cinderella will be glad to see you," Harper said, rising from the floor. She tossed the wipe she was using into the trash.

"Too bad you didn't do that earlier."

"My cleaning schedule exceeds the state guidelines, Miranda. Cinderella is over here. She's the third to come down with some bug. Things spread through children fast."

Miranda scooped up her little girl. "Mamma's got you, Cinderella. Let's get out of this germ fest. Consider this my official notice that I will take her somewhere else from now on."

"Got it. I'll mark that down that your two-week notice starts tomorrow. I'll mail your final bills home. Miranda, I'll share that one of the sick children threw a block at Cinderella. She has a small red mark on her left arm. It's listed on her incident sheet as well as details about her illness for your doctor."

"Someone hurt Cinderella? Really, this place is out of control." Miranda searched for the injury and looked disappointed when she couldn't see it. Exasperated, she looked up at Harper.

"It was right here above her elbow." Harper smoothed a finger over the toddler's arm. "It looks like she's okay now, but there might be a bruise at some point."

Harper's phone buzzed, and she looked at the screen. "This is the parent of the first child who got ill."

After a quick conversation, Harper pushed her phone back into her pocket to report, "I have permission to tell you that Thomas has a virus going around town. I'll write the virus name on the form for Cinderella's doctor."

Breathing a sigh of relief when the unpleasant woman left, Harper reassessed the other children. Everyone seemed fine. *Thank goodness!*

A call notification lit up her cell phone screen. Colt. He wasn't really going to break up with her over the phone, was he? She'd show him. Flipping the phone upside down, she placed it screen down on the flat surface.

Harper needed something to occupy her brain. Pulling her thoughts together, she announced, "Time for art. Let's get your smocks on and we can fingerpaint a picture for your mommies and daddies."

The messy activity took all her supervision and management skills. She didn't notice the frequent buzzing of her phone on the counter. Any calls from the parents would ring out loud.

By the time her day was over and she'd sanitized all the surfaces again, Harper's energy had evaporated. Dragging herself home, she considered what she should have for dinner and decided it was too much effort. Grabbing a soft drink from the refrigerator where Colt had pushed them to the back to discourage her from drinking, Harper stopped in her bedroom to pick up Wombles before settling on the couch to tell him about her day.

"And Miranda announced Cinderella wouldn't return. So, that's one positive, I guess."

Wombles' face expressed all his sympathy about her challenging day.

"Thanks for listening, Wombles. I'm glad you stuck around," Harper bemoaned before looking at her phone. Maybe she should call Amber to check on Rio. When it buzzed again, she almost dropped it in surprise. Forcing herself to be brave, she answered the call.

"Colt, I don't think we have anything to say to each other."

"Are you okay, Angel?"

"Perfect," she proclaimed, sounding as perky as she could manage.

"What is going on, Little girl? I've called fourteen times and left messages. Why are you avoiding me?"

"You'll have to ask your girlfriend. If you're not naked anymore," she snapped.

"The only girl I have in my life is you. Can you tell me what happened?"

"I called to tell you about Rio and the shooting at Murphy's. Your new sweetie answered and told me you didn't want to talk to me and that you were naked," Harper said as she tried to stabilize her voice to keep it from wavering with emotion.

"Damn it! I need to be there to hold you. I do not have a girlfriend, sweetie, or any other romantic partner in my life. I'm trying to figure out who you talked to. Did she sound young?"

"Oh, yeah," Harper confirmed, nodding. "No problem, Colt. I was…silly to believe we could be more than friends. I'm not exciting enough to be part of your life. Don't worry, I won't tell Amber, Maisie, or the guys."

"You are not silly and we are very definitely more than friends. I'll be on a plane tomorrow to come see you."

"Not necessary. Thanks for Wombles. I love him."

"Do not hang up, Little girl," he warned as if he knew what she was planning. "Remember when we created our rules? I asked you to trust me."

After swallowing hard, Harper pressed the screen to disconnect. Hugging Wombles, she checked through her calls to see a message from Amber. Rio had a broken leg and had made it through surgery well.

Relieved that he was going to be okay, Harper texted back a short response, offering her help if she could do anything as her phone buzzed with an incoming call from Colt. With determination, she turned off her phone and picked up the TV remote. She selected her favorite movie—an animated sweet story that ended with her finding her perfect prince.

This time, it felt false. How long could happiness really last?

CHAPTER 17

The next evening, Harper locked the back door to the daycare and turned to walk to her car. Next to her battered sedan sat a large, shiny truck. Colt stepped out and shut the door with a definite push before walking forward.

"Colt? What are you doing here? You have a concert tomorrow in Nashville."

"I do," he confirmed as he stopped in front of her, looking more disheveled than she'd seen him before.

Harper tensed all her muscles, forcing herself to stay in place and not run to him. "Okay, well, safe travels."

"Your bottom is in so much trouble."

"That sounds like a threat, Colt. Should I call the police?"

He stared at her for several long seconds before walking forward. She started backward when he reached her but froze as he wrapped his arms around her to haul her tight against his body. Without saying a word, he buried his face against her neck. Harper felt his warm lips brush her skin softly. Stiffening herself against his warmth, she held her breath to keep his beguiling scent from weakening her resolve.

"I'm sorry you are so hurt. I'd do anything to whisk this doubt from your mind."

"Enough, Colt. I know I always took longer to understand things back in school, but this is pretty simple. We played around for a while and you got bored. It happens."

His hand landed on her bottom in a swift swat that caught her completely by surprise. She bolted forward the scant distance between them only to run into his hard body. "Little girl, you have convinced yourself that something bad happened. It did not."

"Sure. That's why you were naked in a room with a drunk twenty-two-year-old."

"I was in the bathroom in my hotel room. I had left my phone on the bed. My manager came in with his fourth wife, who happens to drink way too much."

"He just came in to hang out with his wife while you were in the shower?" she said skeptically.

"We had a meeting scheduled for a half hour later—just him and me. Why she was there, I don't know."

"You take a shower to smell nice for your manager?" she scoffed, studying his slightly reddish complexion. He even looked guilty.

"I had thirty minutes. That wasn't enough time to talk to you. So, I took a shower while I waited."

"And he had a key to your hotel room?"

"He had my guitar from practice. He needed it for a publicity photo shoot."

"You just have all the answers, don't you?" she demanded, pushing against his chest.

"I have the truth."

"Okay, Colt. You just wallow in the truth."

Harper pushed his shoulders hard, and he let her step back away from him. "See you on Zoom, Colt."

"I'll follow you home."

"I'm going to my apartment alone."

"I'll sit in the hallway until you're ready to talk to me, Little girl."

Harper whirled on her toes and fled to her car. As she jumped in, Colt was there to close her door. Before he pushed it closed, he said sternly, "Do not hurt yourself or others on the way home. Drive carefully. Promise me."

"I promise," popped out of her mouth before she could stop it. Colt shut her door firmly and stepped back. He watched her start the car and drive sedately out of the parking lot before running to jump into his truck.

At the first stoplight, she saw him appear behind her, several vehicles back. He followed her at the same deliberate, safe pace he always did. He made her nervous and much more cautious about driving home. She definitely paid more attention to the old familiar route than she normally did. Sometimes after a long day at work, her car seemed to drive itself home, surprising her when she pulled into a parking spot.

He was right behind her when she reached her apartment and pulled into the space next to her. What was she going to do?

"I really don't want to talk, Colt."

"I know you don't, Angel, but I'm not willing to let you run away. You're too important to me." He followed her inside, shrugging into a jacket that seemed unnecessary for the warm evening.

"Not more important than her."

"I don't even know what her name is, Little girl. I don't care. She's one in a long line of women my manager hooked up with. He knows the music business inside and out but he's clueless about how to choose the right woman. I don't want to talk about either of them."

"You want to talk about us?" she scoffed. "Like there ever has been an us. I'm going inside—without you."

Slamming the door behind her, Harper couldn't keep herself from peeking out the peephole. She watched Colt settle with his back against the wall, his eyes firmly fixed on her door. Afraid he could tell that she was looking, Harper flew away from the door.

Sure he would leave soon, she forced herself to go change clothes. Picking up Wombles in the bedroom, she squeezed the stuffie to her chest. Unable to resist, she tiptoed over to the door and peeked out. Colt had settled down to sit cross-legged on the hall carpet.

As she watched, he rubbed a hand over his face in an undeniable gesture of exhaustion. Her heart broke. He looked like he hadn't slept for days. How did he get here?

That floozy's voice echoed into her mind, "Colt's busy and naked. Stop calling."

Could she have made a mistake? She peeped through the viewer again. Colt's eyes were closed and his head tilted back to rest on the wall behind him. Would he have come all this way if she weren't important to him? Maybe the floozy was important to him, too.

Shaking her head, Harper headed for the kitchen. She needed to get something for dinner. *Has Colt eaten?*

"Stop it!" Harper reprimanded herself.

An hour later, she pushed the remains of the frozen dinner she hadn't taken four bites of down the garbage disposal. Catching sight of Wombles' unapproving glance, Harper crept again to the door. Colt's collar was pulled up around his neck and his arms were wrapped around his torso. Did he look flushed?

Opening the door, she whispered, "Colt? Are you okay?"

"I've got to find Harper. I have to make her understand." His teeth chattered, and he didn't look up at her.

"Colt. You're scaring me. This isn't funny. Just get in your truck and go home."

"Got to get home to Harper. I have to talk to her in person."

"Colt?" Harper inched closer and could feel heat radiating from his body. Tentatively, she pressed her hand against his forehead. "Oh, no. You're burning up, Daddy."

"Daddy. I love to hear you say that, Angel," he mumbled, leaning his cheek against her fingers.

"You're sick, Colt. Let's get you inside. Can you stand, big guy?" She hooked her arm under his and tugged upward. He weighed much more than a toddler.

Several seconds later, Harper was at the point of running to get help from a neighbor's hulking husband when Colt got his feet under himself and stood. She threw an arm around his waist to coax Colt to the door. Twisting the doorknob, she froze. "Crap!" She'd run out, and the door had locked behind her. They couldn't get in.

"This day can't get any worse," she muttered, trying to figure out what to do.

"Best day ever. I'm with you, Little girl," the fevered man mumbled. He carefully brushed her blonde hair from her eyes with his free hand before squeezing her tighter.

"Oh, Daddy. I'm so sorry. I locked us out. I'm trying to remember if I gave a key to anyone I could call. Double crap! I don't have my phone."

"My key's in my pocket, Angel."

Harper met his fevered glance, shocked. "You could have come in any time."

"You needed your space, Little girl." He reached for his keys in his pocket and fumbled around.

Pulling his hand out empty, Colt swayed badly and leaned hard on Harper. "I need to sit down, baby."

Leaning around his powerful frame, Harper pressed a hand into his other pocket and snagged his keyring. Her fingers brushed over a small, velvety box, jolting her heartbeat into overdrive. A thread of hope kindled in her heart.

"Secret," he told her solemnly.

"I won't tell."

Quickly, she forced her mind away from that small jeweler's case and pulled out the keys, finding the blue tinted one she'd had made for Colt. His energy was evaporating and she supported more of his weight with every passing second. She coaxed him to her bedroom and leaned him against the wall for a brief second to throw the covers down to the bottom of the bed.

"Wrong side, Little girl. I need to be closest to the door to take on any threat."

She looked at him in disbelief. Was that why he had claimed his place in her bed? Knowing she couldn't dissuade him, Harper walked him to the other side and Colt collapsed to sit on the edge of the bed.

He toed out of his boots and tugged his pullover jacket and T-shirt up before running out of steam.

Harper quickly freed him from the tangle of material and tried not to stare at the display of muscles that always thrilled her. He stretched out on the bed and turned to curl toward her side of the bed.

"Come to bed, Little girl. I need to hold you. I've missed you so much."

"You need some medicine, Colt." She ran to the bathroom to grab some aspirin and a small cup of water.

"Take these, Colt."

"Daddy's supposed to take care of you," he said sadly. "I've done a very bad job of that."

"Sit up a bit," she urged and helped him take the medicine.

"Thank you, Angel. Come to bed, Little girl. I need to hold you," he repeated.

"I have to take a shower. I'll be right back."

Harper fled into the bathroom and closed the door. Leaning her forehead against cool wood, she inhaled deeply. Exhaling shakily, she tried to pull herself together.

"I'll just take care of him and send him on his way," she promised herself aloud, knowing every syllable of that statement was completely false.

Quickly, she showered and pulled on her baggy nightshirt. After brushing her teeth, Harper opened the door slightly to see Colt sprawled in his jeans on her bed. He had tugged the covers over his bare arms before falling asleep. Her heart immediately skipped a beat at the sight of his hair tousled over his brow. Her fingers itched to stroke it back into place.

Her heart ached. Dashing into the other room, she picked up Wombles from the entry table where she had set him before running out in the hall to check on Colt. Holding him against her heart, she whispered, "I'll explain later." He, of course, understood completely.

Returning to the bedroom, she hesitated. She could go sleep on the couch.

"Come here, Little girl."

Unable to resist, she crawled into bed and hugged the side to put space between them.

"Eep!"

He wrapped an arm around her waist and pulled her tight against his body before snaking his hand under her shirt to span her ribcage just under her breast.

"Mine," he whispered before tumbling back into sleep.

CHAPTER 18

*H*arper kept her eye on her phone the next morning at the daycare. All the students were back and feeling fine. The under twenty-four-hour illness had quickly run its way through the impacted kids.

When she'd snuck a hand over Colt's forehead that morning as he slept, his temperature had dissipated, to her relief. Dressing quickly, she'd grabbed her sunflower butter toast before letting herself out of the apartment. As Harper drove away, she regretted not leaving a note.

What would I have said? I slept better in your arms than I have since you left?

Every time that black box popped into her mind, she pushed it away, refusing to let herself dream that he had bought it for her. Her phone began to buzz out of control with a series of messages.

I love you.

I only love you.

I only love you, my precious Angel.

I only love you, my precious Angel, my Little girl.

A stupid man would screw that up. An intelligent one would cherish our relationship forever.

Consider this: I waited years to have sex because the time wasn't right with you. When it is, do you think I'd become so sex crazed that I'd go on a binge with anyone?

Holding her breath, she waited for the next message, but nothing appeared. Cursing him mentally, Harper flipped her phone upside down so she couldn't see the screen. Even as she debated the ridiculous idea that the guy she'd known since third grade would have transformed into a sex maniac after making love with her, of all people, Harper felt relieved that he was obviously feeling better. *Thank goodness.*

By the end of the day, she was antsy not knowing what she'd find at home. The parents picked up their children and wished her a happy weekend. When she pulled into the parking lot at the apartment complex, a limo was parked in front of her building. Grousing slightly at whoever was lucky enough to live a limousine life, Harper parked a distance from her door.

Walking slowly past, she admired the sleek vehicle. She'd never ridden in one. To her surprise, a man wearing a black suit stepped out of the car.

He smiled and asked, "Harper Benson?"

"Yes?"

"I'm Jerry, your driver. Colt Ziegler requests you join him at his concert. He asked that you call him."

"Colt? Oh, I can't go to a concert," she automatically refused.

"Give him a call," Jerry suggested.

"Okay," she agreed hesitantly.

Turning to face her building for a bit of privacy, Harper juggled her things to select his number. She tried not to think about the last call she'd made to him as it connected. At the sound of his deep voice, she felt her shoulders settle back into place.

"Harper. Change into jeans and that pretty pink top. Pack a bag for the weekend and jump in the limo. Jerry will take you to the airport."

"Colt, I can't just leave," she protested.

"You don't work until Monday, right?"

"Right..."

"Bring one of your pretty dresses. I want to show you the town. Move quickly. The plane's leaving in an hour."

"I can't get packed and to the airport. It will take an hour to get checked in," she pointed out, shaking her head even though he couldn't see it. "Besides..."

"Trust me, Little girl. I'm taking care of you just as you took care of your Daddy last night. Come, let me show you that you are the only one I'd ever consider letting into my life. You need to see the truth to believe it."

Opening her mouth to argue, Harper snapped it shut. He was right. She'd never just take his word to reject the suspicion in her mind.

"Go pack."

She stared at the blank phone screen. Colt had hung up. Harper looked up to meet Jerry's gaze. At his smile, she decided. "I'll be right back."

"I'll be here, miss."

Dashing inside, Harper threw off her baby-stained clothes and pulled on a fresh pair of jeans and the pink shirt he'd requested. As she fastened the buttons, Harper felt pleased that he had even noticed what she was wearing. This was one of her favorites as well.

She threw underwear, socks, another pair of jeans, and a couple of T-shirts, as well as her second favorite dress from her shopping expedition into a suitcase. After doing what she could to make herself look presentable, she quickly gathered a small amount of makeup and daringly tucked the last couple of condoms from Colt's box into her suitcase. Adding her one pair of high heels, Harper zipped it up.

She grabbed her purse as she retraced her steps to the limo. Jerry placed her small roller case into the trunk before Harper could change her mind and ushered her into the palatial back seat. A fragrant bouquet of roses sat inside in one cupholder. Leaning forward automatically to sniff, Harper saw a white card tucked into the blossoms.

I love you, Little girl, today and all our tomorrows.

Harper tried to keep her heart from becoming hopeful as she clasped her hands to her chest. Colt had been the only one to give her roses, starting with a pink one at Valentine's Day in the sixth grade. She sat back as Jerry maneuvered the long vehicle out of the parking lot.

Am I really doing this?

Stiffening her resolve, Harper knew she needed to find out for sure. Living without Colt had been like having her heart ripped from her chest. Seeing him so sick last night had suggested maybe he needed her as much as she needed him. An idea kindled inside her mind.

That thought fled as Jerry turned onto a small road instead of getting on the highway to head to the nearest town with an airport. Opening her mouth to suggest he'd missed a turn, she fell silent when he went through a gated entrance. To her surprise, Harper saw a small plane sitting on a runway ahead. This small airstrip wasn't a secret in town, but only the rich man who owned this land used it. She scanned the area looking for the famous person who that plane awaited.

When Jerry stopped a short distance away, she asked, "Are we picking someone else up?"

"The plane will take you the rest of the way."

"I'm going on that?"

"Yes, miss. Let me open your door and we'll get you on your way."

She paused as she got out and scooped up the vase and flowers. Harper wasn't leaving those behind. She walked forward slowly, lagging behind Jerry who rolled her suitcase to the luggage hatch below.

"Hello, Harper. You're quick. We were expecting it would take you an hour to pack. Come in," a friendly voice called from the doorway. "I'm Pete. I'll be your pilot today."

"Hi!" Harper climbed the steps and let Pete take the flowers from her when he promised to keep them safe during the flight. Another man in the cockpit called hello, and she returned the greeting before following the pilot to a luxurious seat and sitting down.

"That's Tom. He's taking care of the preflight communication with the tower. We'll be off in a few. You'll need to stay in your seat during take-off and landing. It should be a smooth flight so you can get up and wander around while in the air. The toilet is in the back."

"Thanks. I'll just stay here," she promised as she buckled her seat-belt, not sure about the small plane. She'd only ridden on a plane twice.

Harper watched him disappear out the door and heard a bang. *He's just stowing my luggage*, she thought. When he reappeared, Pete entered the open door of the cockpit and slid into his chair to put on his head-set. She watched with fascination as he flipped levers and pushed buttons before taking the wheel and driving the plane down the runway.

Quickly, they lifted into the air. Staring out the window, Harper had fun seeing the tops of familiar buildings as they headed out of town. When she realized she'd pressed her nose against the immacu-late window, she sat back to wipe her print off.

She hadn't even asked how long the flight was. Looking around, she marveled at the interior of the small plane. Brushing her hand over the soft leather of the seat below her, Harper imagined she was rich and got to jet-set anywhere she wanted to go.

Colt organized this. This must be his life now.

It was mind-boggling that the down-to-earth boy she'd loved for as long as she could remember lived a lifestyle like this. He didn't seem any different, but maybe that was only because they knew each other so well. Harper knew she'd see how being famous had impacted Colt's personality soon.

"Would you like a glass of wine?" Tom offered, suddenly appearing at her side.

"Oh, no. I don't want to put you to any trouble. I'll just sit here, I'm fine."

"They'll fire me if I don't do something to earn my keep. You don't want that to happen."

"Oh, no. O-kay, I can drink a small glass of wine."

"I'll be right back."

Soon, he sat a glass in front of her with a blush wine and a selec-tion of cheeses and crackers. Self-consciously, Harper took a sip of the wine as if she knew everything about it. "It's delicious," she announced.

"Great. Just let me know if you'd like anything else."

"Okay. Thank you, Tom."

"You're welcome." He grabbed a couple of bottles of water and returned to the cockpit.

When her stomach growled, reminding her she'd eaten lunch hours ago, Harper helped herself to the beautiful display. Her eyes rolled up in delight at the yummy flavor of the creamy cheese and crisp crackers. The food and beverage combination was incredible together.

Happily, she finished her snack without worrying about leaving some so Tom wouldn't be appalled at her lack of control. She'd never be on a private plane again and she was starving. To her delight, the empty plate was replaced by a hot cookie.

"More wine?"

"Could I have a bottle of water, please?"

"Of course," Tom said, clearing the small table beside her and returning with a cold bottle of fancy water.

With a full tummy including a glass of wine, Harper laid her head back against the headrest and reclined the seat slightly. She stared out the window at the puffy clouds and wondered how Colt could ever prove to her that the woman who'd answered her phone meant nothing to him. Without finding the answers in the blue sky, she drifted to sleep.

When Tom woke her, a flurry of activities followed. After landing, a driver ushered her into the back seat of a massive SUV. He expertly navigated through a crush of cars, signs proclaiming Colt's name, and security gates to reach the backdoor of the arena. Promising he would take care of her luggage, the driver escorted her to the door.

"Hey, Harper! I'm so excited to meet you. I'm with Colt's PR firm. Put this lanyard around your neck. It has your backstage pass. You got here just in time. Colt's getting ready to go on. Let's get you to the side stage so you can watch."

Just then, a huge roar of excitement sounded from the gathered masses. Unable to hear the man in front of her, she accepted his arm and allowed him to guide her past a flurry of backstage workers and equipment. He steadied her when she tripped over a coil of electric cords. She looked up to see Colt jamming out on stage.

"Damn, he looks edible," she thought as her guide stationed her by a tall stack of crates where she'd be out of the way and protected. She devoured Colt with her gaze as he entertained the crowd. The audience sang his songs, sending the concert back at Colt and the band. What an amazing feeling as a singer and composer to have people love your words so much they memorized every note!

A movement beside her drew her attention from his powerful body. Her escort stood a small distance away and waved his arms up and down. The movement caught Colt's attention. Instantly, the handsome musician focused on Harper. His smile changed from sparkling to devastating as he looked at her.

"So, you're Harper?" a familiar voice asked.

Harper turned to see a young woman. Her expression was hard and devoid of friendliness or happiness. The jewelry lavished over her stylishly thin frame was blinding and to Harper, overkill. If there had been a picture in the dictionary of a gold-digger, this woman would be perfect. Harper could have kicked herself. She would have thrown away everything for this woman? Colt would never be attracted to her.

"Hi. You're the fourth wife, right?" Harper asked with a relieved smile.

"What?" The woman glared at her before warning, "He'll tire of you."

"Maybe, but he'll never be interested in you," Harper stated, standing up for herself. She turned to look back at the stage and found Colt watching her as he sang. She could read the concern in his gaze even from this distance away. He held one finger up to ask her to wait for a second. Harper felt the malevolent presence of the woman who'd answered the phone slink away.

As soon as that song was finished, he announced to the audience that he would be right back. Dashing to her side, he kissed her fiercely

145

before running back on stage. "My Angel's backstage tonight. I've waited a long time for it to be our time."

The crowd roared its approval, making Harper smile. These were his people. His fans. She loved that he had created such a bond through sharing his music.

He talked about the next song as Harper half-listened. She focused more on his band, who all waved her way and seemed happy to see her. When the notes sounded, she met Colt's gaze and watched him extend a hand in invitation. It was their song. The one they'd always sang at Murphy's. She looked at the crowd and shook her head. *I can't go out there.*

"Trust me, Angel. Join me," he requested firmly.

Shocked as the crowd chanted "Angel, Angel, Angel," Harper found her feet walking forward, carrying her body toward him. The audience hushed as she appeared at the side of the stage. She knew what they were thinking—how could she be what Colt wanted?

"Come on, Angel. I can't do this alone." He nodded to the band, and she realized that they'd repeated the intro several times to give him time to coax her forward. This time, they continued into the first verse.

Harper leaned into the microphone that she swore smelled like him. Keeping her eyes on him, she sang. Her voice warbled a bit, but steadied and strengthened as he smiled at her. When Colt leaned forward to sing the joint chorus together, she loved the heat of his skin millimeters from hers.

The hush that had fallen over the crowd broke as a few people chanted "Angel" once again. When her chorus arrived, they hooted and hollered as she confidently brought the most from the familiar notes. She channeled her love for Colt into the song and loved the feel of his hand stroking over her back briefly before returning to the neck of his guitar.

When the song ended, she felt like she heard the combined inhale of the crowd before they erupted in cheers and wild applause.

"That's my Angel, folks. She's pretty special, isn't she?"

The band members all nodded and chimed in with their agreement. Harper didn't know what to say. Flustered, she leaned into the mic and said, "Thank you for loving my... Colt." Glancing back at Colt, she made sure he wasn't mad that she'd almost said Daddy as the crowd reacted to her words. She looked back at the sheltered spot where she'd stood in the beginning.

"Go, Angel," he whispered for her ears only. "I love you."

With a wave at the crowd, she exited the lit stage and took refuge in the shadows. She felt ridiculously proud of herself. As he continued the concert, Harper relaxed against the crates and basked in his music. They were fantastic in person. The band's talent sounded very close to the polished, professional performances recorded in a studio.

If he was as tired as the illness-affected children in her care, Harper couldn't tell. Colt and his band were putting on a phenomenal show. If she were here for nothing else, seeing her Daddy in his element was totally worth it.

CHAPTER 19

*W*aking up the next morning in Colt's arms, Harper cuddled closer to his body. She smiled at the feel of his lips pressed against her hair. Colt had made slow, devastatingly sweet love to her last night. There was no mistaking the emotional connection they shared. He was her person. Her everything. Her Daddy.

"I love you, Little girl."

"I love you, too, Daddy. I'm sorry I caused us to lose time."

"You didn't cause anything. But I need you to promise that you'll tell me if something disturbing happens and listen to what I say."

"That's hard sometimes because people don't always tell the truth."

"I will never lie to you, Angel."

Harper thought back over the years that they'd known each other. He hadn't ever told her something that wasn't true, even when it would have been easier. She should have remembered that earlier. Turning her face into his chest, she hid from him.

"Stop, Harper. You didn't cause the problem. Had I taken my phone into the bathroom with me, none of this would have occurred," Colt pointed out.

"It's not your fault she answered your phone." Harper lifted her head to meet his gaze to challenge that statement.

"Then we agree. This is all on whatever her name is."

"You still don't know?" Harper asked and giggled.

"I don't and it's fine. My manager's track record isn't good. She'll be working on her next husband soon. Enough of her. Let's talk about us."

"I like that—us."

"Me, too. We meet with the architect together on Friday evening. Did I tell you I figured out who our neighbors are?"

"Really? Who?"

"Amber and Rio."

"Amber and Rio? Oh! I forgot to tell you the reason I called you in the first place. A man started shooting in Murphy's. Rio took him down but broke his leg," Harper shared.

"What? At Murphy's? How's Rio?" Colt asked.

"He had surgery. They expect him to make a full recovery. There's a surprise party for him on Wednesday."

"And we'll go."

"Do you have time?" she asked, feeling hopeful.

"I'll make time. Our friends are important."

"I'm really glad they're going to be our neighbors," Harper celebrated.

"Me, too. Now, we just need to get Maisie and Beau back into town."

"You never know. Maybe they'll choose some land near us as well."

"That would be miraculous, Little girl. Just don't get your heart too set on it. I'd hate for you to be disappointed," he warned.

Puckering her lips, Harper distracted him with a quick kiss. She leaned back to look at his handsome face. Loving the flare of passion in his expression, Harper traced the skiff of hair that led down the center line of his torso. "Can I touch you, Daddy?"

"You have my permission, Little girl. I would love to feel your hand around me."

Tentatively, she drew a line along the upper side of his morning erection. Exploring his shaft, she wrapped her fingers around him and squeezed lightly, drawing a groan from Colt.

"Lick your hand, Angel."

Harper loved the heat radiating from his eyes as she lifted her hand to her lips. Feeling dangerous, she lapped up her palm over her fingers, and watched his eyes darken as they focused on her actions. She felt daring, sexy, and powerful all wrapped into one, loving the heady feeling.

Returning her hand to its former grip, she slid her hand down his thick cock. His hand wrapped around hers, showing her how to please him. Daringly, she leaned down to lap at the head when it emerged from her grip. The buck of his hips told her everything she needed to know. She set out to drive him crazy.

* * *

BACK AT HOME on Sunday afternoon, Harper tried to do all her weekend stuff in a couple of hours. Colt pitched in to complete the chores and limited the number of things Harper thought she needed to do. Making a list, he promised he would work on them while he was at home that week.

Harper didn't argue. She felt awful. Her period was overdue and she felt nauseous when she smelled certain scents. Why would powdered laundry detergent make her sick? That fresh scent the manufacturer added made her lurch for the sink, sure she would lose her lunch.

She couldn't be pregnant, could she? They'd used condoms every time. Colt made sure to protect her. What would he say? Channeling her inner Maisie, she figured out how to get to the store to buy a test. Her no-nonsense brilliant friend would point out that was the only way Harper would know.

Remembering the TV shows she'd seen that tested in the morning, Harper pretended to potty when her Daddy sent her to the toilet when she woke up. Feeling like she would burst, Harper stopped at the twenty-four-hour store on her way to the daycare. Harper couldn't decide quickly which test to buy. Panicking that she'd have an accident, she picked up three different ones and paid for them quickly.

She opened the packages at the first stoplight and started reading the directions. Colt would kill her for doing anything other than paying attention while in the car. Harper tried to rationalize that she wasn't reading while driving. She knew that wouldn't be good enough for her Daddy. That didn't stop her from making sure she knew what to do.

Dashing into the bathroom, she readied all the tests while dancing with the need to use the toilet. Finally, she peed on all the sticks, fumbling one into the toilet. "Crap!"

A knock on the door told her time was up. It still was early, but the parents would know that she was there. Quickly finishing her business, Harper threw the spoiled tester in the trash and washed her hands. She stored the others in the cabinet above the toilet to finish processing and dashed out to open the door.

Miranda stood in the doorway. Just what Harper needed.

"I read my contract. You have to give me two weeks to find a new provider."

"Correct. Good morning, Cinderella. You're here first. Would you like to help me get ready for our first activity?"

Sighing loudly, Miranda rebuked her, "Putting the kids to work? Really, Harper. That is incredibly lazy."

"Here, Cinderella. You put the circles on the floor in a big O for our share time. Do you know what an O looks like?"

When the little girl held up her hands over her head to make an O just like they'd practiced, Harper handed the colorful circles to Cinderella.

"Thank you very much," Harper said cheerfully to the toddler who was looking back and forth between the adults and trying to figure out if she should get upset. Distracted by the rubber items in her hands, she toddled off happily to put them in a pattern that didn't resemble any letter of the alphabet at all.

"Miranda, if you are unpleasant, I can void the contract at any time. Feel free to reread the contract. I will not warn you again."

Harper stood straight and looked her directly in the eyes. She was done with being Miranda's punching bag.

"Your mother would be appalled at you speaking to me like this."

"On the contrary, she'll cheer when I tell her I just dropped your grace period to find a new daycare to one week. Yes, I can do that. Feel free to choose to start today."

"I never," Miranda huffed and walked to the door.

When the little girl returned to Harper's side and looked up at her, Harper praised her efforts. After asking her to find all the blue stuffies in the bin, Harper ran to the bathroom to check the results.

Two pink lines and the word 'pregnant' looked back at her. What would Colt say? How was she going to tell him?

CHAPTER 20

"What's going on with you, Harper? You don't seem yourself," Colt asked on Wednesday as they got ready for Rio's surprise party.

"I'm just tired."

"We'll come home early from the party so you can go to sleep before your normal bedtime," Colt decreed.

"Let's stay long enough to talk to Amber and Rio. I haven't talked to her since she started her new job."

"Talk quickly."

Harper nodded. She knew she had put a distance between herself and Colt. Keeping secrets was so hard for her. Especially from people she loved.

She felt Amber's eyes on her several times at the party. Harper tried to act normal but knew her friend could sense something was wrong. With a smile on her face, Harper tried to act normally.

When they slipped away into the crowd to head home early, Harper ran into Mr. Murphy. She tried to just smile and slip away but he wanted to talk.

"Harper, you know my baby well. Do you think Rio is good enough for her?"

"I think Rio is exactly what Amber needs to make her happy. I know she'd love it if you'd welcome him fully into the family," Harper said, trying to help her friend.

"I guess she's old enough to make up her own mind," Mr. Murphy said, looking across the room at Amber sitting as close as possible to Rio with his arm around her shoulders. "He always was a good guy. I guess I need to forget he's older than her."

"Yes, sir. That would be my suggestion," Colt added.

"Thanks. I'm glad to see the two of you together. I always thought you'd make a perfect family," Amber's father said offhandedly before walking away.

A family? Tears filled her eyes as she was overwhelmed by emotions. Harper turned and ran from the bar.

"Whoa!" Colt wrapped his arms around her waist when she reached the parking lot and lifted her off her feet to protect Harper from an approaching car.

Feeling the air brush by her, Harper stared into Colt's eyes, frightened to the core by what she almost did. "The baby!" she whispered frantically, putting her hand over her abdomen.

"The baby? Are you pregnant, Little girl?" he asked, scanning her face. Releasing one arm from around her, he covered Harper's hand over her stomach as if providing extra protection to the life inside her.

"Yes. I'm so scared."

"I should spank your bottom until you can't sit down for not telling me immediately. I'll wait until we get home from the doctor's office."

Wrapping his arms around her, Colt whirled her around in a circle, celebrating with as much enthusiasm as Harper remembered when he scored the winning touchdown to win the state title. When he set her gently down on her feet, Colt kissed her tenderly.

"You're happy?" she asked when he lifted his head.

"I'm ecstatic, over the moon, on cloud nine." His expression became concerned. "How do you feel about having a baby?"

Harper rubbed her stomach before looking up at Colt. "I'm scared and excited. I love this baby already. It's part of you."

Colt covered her hand on her abdomen and paused for a second. "Angel, she'll be the most precious gift on Earth."

"You mean he, right? I'm pretty sure this is a boy."

"I don't think so," Colt teased before sobering. "First, we make sure you're healthy, then we make plans. Looks like we'll need two nurseries in our new house."

"Colt, can I be your Little girl if we have a child running around?"

"Of course you can. We'll be discreet, but you'll always be my Little girl. Nothing will change that," he assured her. He hugged her close, and they stood silently together for several long seconds. She loved being close to him and suspected that his thoughts mirrored her own —wondering at the change in their lives since the reunion.

"Let's go home and talk," he suggested. "We'll celebrate with a glass of milk."

"I'd love that."

On the way home, Harper commented, "Rio and Amber looked so happy. She glowed. I'm glad her father is adjusting his attitude toward their relationship. He really only wanted her to be happy."

Colt linked his fingers with hers and squeezed gently. "When are you going to tell them?"

"After we see the doctor. I think it will seem more real then."

"Definitely. I want to be there with you," he stressed. "I know it's tough juggling schedules."

"It's hard for me to get away from the daycare, too. We'll make it work. I'm going to call Rose to see if she'll work part time until we get the new center built and then full time."

"That's a great idea. You'll have a flood of parents trying to secure a place for their child. You'll need more staff. I won't let you exhaust yourself," he warned.

"Yes, Daddy," she said without hesitation and smiled at her automatic response.

"What are you thinking, Angel?"

"I can't believe this is actually working out. That we're together… And you're my Daddy."

"You may not be so happy about that when we get home."

Harper turned in her seat to look at him. "I'm sorry I didn't tell you immediately."

"There can't be any secrets between us, Angel. With me on the road from time to time, it's easy to have something blow up into a big problem."

"I know."

"Shoulda, coulda, woulda, Little girl. No regrets from now on," he said sternly.

"Yes, Daddy. Are you going to spank me?"

"I think I have a better way of reminding you to talk to me," he suggested. "I picked up a special case for you while I was on the road."

"Like a suitcase?"

"Not quite, Angel." Colt pulled into the parking lot and backed into a space before coming around to help her out.

She clung to his hand as they walked into the apartment. Harper hated to admit, even to herself, that she could feel the wetness gathering between her thighs. The discipline that Colt lavished on her made her feel loved and protected. He always rewarded her for being good.

"I'll be good from now on," she promised as he shut the door, sealing the rest of the world out.

"I'm glad to hear that, Angel." He steered her to the bedroom and next to the bed.

Kneeling in front of her, Colt slipped off her shoes and socks. Unfastening her pants, he slid that garment and her panties down her legs and helped her step out of them. "Lean over the bed to lie on your tummy, Little girl."

Slowly, she followed his directions and waited. She could hear him moving around and his footsteps as he returned to her side before placing a hard plastic case on the bed. Holding her breath as he opened it, Harper gasped at the sight of two rows of ever larger plugs nestled inside.

"Can't I get a second chance?" she whispered.

Colt opened the top of a bottle of lubricant with a distinctive click. She understood she would not escape from her actions. He plucked the smallest plug from the case and set it on the bed in her line of vision. Harper jumped when he stroked a hand over her bare bottom.

"Relax, Angel. It will make it easier on you."

She tried not to clench her bottom as he spread her buttocks to reveal that small hidden entrance. The feel of the cool, slick liquid on her skin made her tighten her muscles to prevent his invasion.

"No!" she whimpered as his finger spread the lubricant and then pushed inside slowly.

"Did you tell Daddy the truth immediately?"

"No…"

"Were you making yourself sick with worry?"

When she didn't answer, not wanting to incriminate herself, he repeated the question. This time, she nodded and felt him withdraw his finger, only to press two inside her next. Harper closed her eyes as they scissored inside her, stretching her tight entrance.

This shouldn't be arousing!

"Daddy's neglected you, Angel."

"No. I mean—that's okay. You don't need to do anything to my bottom."

He just chuckled. The low sound of his amused laughter sent shivers down her spine. There was no mistaking the message.

She watched Colt pick up the plug and soon felt the cold metal against her. Her efforts to keep him out were futile, and it glided inside her bottom until the base rested firmly against her. She shivered at the feel of the chilly object stretching her passageway.

"Let me clean my hands and we'll go celebrate with our milk."

"Wearing this?" she squeaked.

"You'll get used to having your bottom full, Little girl." He leaned over to kiss her cheek before moving away.

Never!

Soon, she wiggled as she sat on the couch with Wombles, waiting for Colt to return with the milk. The plug pressed deeper inside her in this position. "Maybe I should go lie down," she suggested as he returned.

"Soon, I'll put you to bed." Colt set the glasses on the side table before sitting next to her and scooping her onto his lap. His hard thigh under her pushed the device even further, making her squirm to move back to the soft padding of the seat.

"Stay where you are," he warned, bouncing his knee.

"Oh!" Immediately, she sat still.

Colt handed her the milk and clinked their glasses together as if they were drinking fine champagne. "Cheers, Little girl. Here's to an amazing future together for our family."

He shifted slightly to work the small velvet box out of his pocket. "I've carried this around for too long, Angel. Will you marry me?"

Harper's heart leapt inside her chest and tears coursed from her eyes to run down her face. His fingers, callused from hours of playing the guitar, gently wiped the moisture from her cheeks as he looked at her in concern.

"We can wait until you're ready," he quietly suggested.

"No! I think it's just the hormones. I'm so emotional."

"Will you marry me, Harper Benson?"

"Yes!" She watched him pull the ring from the box and hoped with all her might that it wouldn't be too small. To her delight, he slid it easily onto her finger.

"It's big, but your fingers may swell during your pregnancy. We'll get it resized after the baby gets here," he suggested as she held out her hand to stare at the sparkling stones.

"It's gorgeous! I love it. Wombles does, too."

"I'm glad you both approve of my selection," he said with a smile before kissing her lips softly.

"We'll get matching silicone rings made for us to wear to work. I know you don't want to scratch someone. Do you want a big wedding?"

"No. All those people would make me nervous. To tell you the truth, I'd love to get married in one of my pretty dresses. I have an ivory one left. I think it would look nice."

"I think that sounds perfect, Angel."

"A judge at the courthouse could marry us in front of a few friends and family members soon, so I still fit into it. I don't want to wait anymore."

"If that's what you want..."

Harper nodded enthusiastically. "It is, Daddy."

"Then that's what we'll do. We'll make an appointment and notify Amber, Rio, Maisie, and Beau."

"Do you think they'll ever end up together?"

"Maisie and Beau?" he asked.

"Yes. I know they still feel the same way about each other."

"I think Beau has waited long enough for his Little girl. This time, he won't take no for an answer."

When Harper opened her mouth to argue, Colt simply bounced her on his knee and her mouth snapped shut with a click of teeth.

"Let's just send good thoughts their way. Have you told your parents?"

"No. No one."

"We'll go see them soon and share our news. For now, I just want to keep you all to myself to enjoy."

He plucked the empty glass from her hand, setting the drinkware on the side table. Leaning back, Colt hooked her knees over his and spread his legs to widen hers. "I think a brave Little girl who tells her Daddy the truth deserves a reward, don't you?" he asked, stroking his fingers through the wetness between her legs.

"Oh, yes, Daddy," she answered, setting Wombles on the couch so he couldn't see.

EPILOGUE

"Colt and Harper look so happy," Maisie whispered, trying not to cry as her best friends stood in front of the judge, reciting their vows. She leaned against the man next to her, drawing on his strength.

"It's our time next, Little girl," Beau answered, squeezing her tighter.

"Like that's ever going to happen. You're still a public figure and I'm that girl from the wrong side of the tracks."

The ceremony concluded, and the couple turned to face those dearest to them. Applause filled the room, making it impossible for Beau to answer. A short time later, they congratulated Colt and Harper together.

"It only took eleven thousand, three hundred and two days to make her mine," Colt reported with a smile, making Harper laugh that he'd counted all the days from the beginning of third grade.

"Did Wombles get to see?" she asked Maisie.

"He peeked out to watch," her friend reassured her with a pat to the tote bag over her shoulder.

"So, you're the last ones left," Colt pointed out.

"Not everyone gets a fairytale ending," Maisie answered bluntly.

"They do if they're good," Beau corrected.

"Right," she agreed sarcastically.

"It appears your brilliant mind has one more lesson to learn. But don't mind us, Colt and Harper. We're so happy for you both."

"Completely ecstatic. You two were always in perfect harmony. I've seen the video of you singing together at the concert. Will you join Colt on tour, Harper?"

"No. I have big plans here. I might join him on special occasions. It wasn't as petrifying as I thought it would be. I guess having Colt there made it less scary."

"That's a good sign that you're with the right person," Colt commented. "Hold on a minute." He ran over to retrieve a large packet. "This needs to spend time with you now. I'll ask to borrow it again."

Maisie peered in to see the tattered pages of the book they'd all shared. It reminded her instantly of all her teenage hopes and dreams. The hole in her life she tried to ignore gaped a bit wider. To cover her thoughts, she said, "Wow, that seems so long ago."

"Thank you, Colt. I'd love to reread it," Beau said, accepting the package.

"It's probably safer if I hold on to it," Maisie pointed out, wanting to keep it close.

"I'm sure we can come to a diplomatic solution. Especially since I'm staying with you while I'm in DC," Beau pointed out.

"That's great news," Harper chimed as Rio and Amber joined them.

"What's good news?" Amber asked quickly.

"Maisie and Beau are moving in together," Harper shared.

The others shook their heads. Harper never could keep a secret. Well, not for long.

Thank you for reading Shoulda: A Second Chance For Mr. Right!

Don't miss future sweet and steamy Daddy stories by Pepper North? Subscribe to my newsletter!

I'm excited to offer you a glimpse into Woulda, the next story in the A Second Chance For Mr. Right series!

Woulda: A Second Chance For Mr. Right
Chapter One

"I expected that after high school was over, you'd stop spending time with that crew of yours," Beau's father pronounced at breakfast a month after graduation.

"They're my friends, Dad," Beau answered evenly.

"It's time to move on from school chums, Beau. You have a potential career ahead of you in politics. Everyone will watch your every move now. What you do. Who you associate with."

"I appreciate the warning, Dad, but I'll be honest. This isn't a negotiable item. I'll go to the school you've picked out. I'll participate in the right social events. I won't abandon my friends."

The look on his father's face hardened as between what he knew his family expected of him and his own needs and desires. He took a deep breath and exhaled silently as his father considered him, letting the time stretch between them to increase the pressure on his son.

"I would like you to reconsider, Beau. There are certain standards that are expected by people at our social level."

"I understand that, Dad."

"The girl who's going to nursing school—she's a good constituent to interact with. The others will not help your base. Especially that homeless girl."

"None of my friends are homeless, Dad. If you're talking about Maisie, she's brilliant. It is very possible that she will revolutionize science in the future. That sounds like an excellent person to stay in contact with," Beau pointed out, knowing that any argument was futile.

"Good for her. I'm glad she's used her brains to grab a scholarship. Family background never changes, son. She's not at your level... socially. And that's what people will judge you for."

Beau shook his head and watch anger flare in his father's eyes before the senator reined it back under control. "I'm sorry, Dad. This isn't a negotiable item with me. Maisie is my friend. I plan for her to be more than that in the future. You can hope that my relationships with my friends will disappear as we scatter away from Avondale, but I'll fight against that happening with every fiber of my being."

"Beau, listen to your father. He is simply trying to guide you so you don't make any mistakes that endanger your future career," Beau's mother spoke for the first time.

"Thank you, Mother. I understand that," Beau answered without changing his mind. Nothing his parents said could make him lose his friends.

"I don't understand your attitude, young man. I hoped your mother and I had raised you better. Time will tell. This conversation may have been totally unnecessary. School day friendships don't survive as time passes," Senator Granville advised.

"I'll keep that in mind, Dad," Beau answered politely as he stood and placed his napkin on the table next to his half-eaten breakfast. Some-how, he wasn't hungry anymore.

"Harrumph."

At the sound of his father's disbelief that he had taken to heart the warning, Beau maintained his pleasant expression and exited the room. Once away from his parents' observation, he headed for the garage, shaking his head. At the back door, the cook handed him two hastily made breakfast sandwiches and bottles of water.

"Thanks, Adele. You're the best."

"You tell Maisie, hi, for me."

"I'll do it."

Smiling at how much the long-time cook understood about their household, Beau headed for his convertible. He didn't have a date with Maisie, but he knew she'd spend her time at the library today. It was the best place for her to study now that graduation had passed. To his delight, he ran into her only a couple of blocks from her house.

"Hey! Want a ride?" Beau called, pulling next to the curb.

"Don't you have world domination to take care of?" she asked, holding a stack of tattered books in front of her.

"That's on my planner for later. Now, I get to spend time with my girl."

Maisie rolled her eyes and got into the car. "You are so full of it."

Want to read more? One-click Woulda: A Second Chance For Mr. Right!

* * *

Read more from Pepper North

Dr. Richards' Littles®

A beloved age play series that features Littles who find their forever
Daddies and Mommies. Dr. Richards guides and supports their efforts
to keep their Littles happy and healthy.
Available on Amazon

Dr. Richards' Littles®
is a registered trademark of
With A Wink Publishing, LLC.
All rights reserved.

SANCTUM

Pepper North introduces you to an age play community that is isolated from the surrounding world. Here Littles can be Little, and Daddies can care for their Littles and keep them protected from the outside world.

Available on Amazon

Soldier Daddies

What private mission are these elite soldiers undertaking? They're all
searching for their perfect Little girl.
Available on Amazon

The Keepers

This series from Pepper North is a twist on contemporary age play romances. Here are the stories of humans cared for by specially selected Keepers of an alien race. These are science fiction novels that age play readers will love!

Available on Amazon

The Magic of Twelve

The Magic of Twelve features the stories of twelve women transported on their 22nd birthday to a new life as the droblin (cherished Little one) of a Sorcerer of Bairn. These magic wielders have waited a long time to take complete care of their droblin's needs. They will protect their precious one to their last drop of magic from a growing menace. Each novel is a complete story.

Available on Amazon

Ever just gone for it? That's what *USA Today* Bestselling Author
Pepper North did in 2017 when she posted a book for sale on
Amazon without telling anyone. Thanks to her amazing fans, the
support of the writing community, Mr. North, and a killer schedule,
she has now written more than 80 books!
Enjoy contemporary, paranormal, dark, and erotic romances that are
both sweet and steamy? Pepper will convert you into one of her loyal
readers. What's coming in the future? A Daddypalooza!

Sign up for Pepper North's newsletter

Like Pepper North on Facebook

Join Pepper's Readers' Group for insider information and giveaways!

Follow Pepper everywhere!

Amazon Author Page
BookBub
FaceBook
GoodReads
Instagram
TikToc
Twitter
YouTube
Visit Pepper's website for a current checklist of books!

Printed in Great Britain
by Amazon

20752121R00102